PRAISE

"THE CRADLE OF ETERNAL NIGHT encapsulates both the beauty and terror of sapphic love at its purest. Two wayward souls forcing love to bloom in the most inhospitable of conditions, under a bleak and unyielding darkness that seems hopeless to penetrate. Ladz keeps you on tenterhooks wondering how Hanka and Basia could possibly prevail through this brutal landscape before delivering you to the sweet promise of a romantic end."

—**Camilla Andrew**, author of
THE ESSENCE OF THE EQUINOX trilogy

"THE CRADLE OF ETERNAL NIGHT asks the question of if love can exist in a Bloodborne-esque world of darkness, corruption, and monsters, and you'll be pleased to know the answer is a resoundingly sapphic YES. This is a dark treat for those who take their romantasy with a spoonful of monster flesh. You'll come back begging for second-helpings, I promise."

— **T.D. Cloud**, author of *OSSUARY* and *INFAUST*

"THE CRADLE OF ETERNAL NIGHT is imaginative and darkly beautiful. Ladz seamlessly blends lurid horror, dark fantasy, and sapphic romance. Perfect for fans of the eerie aspects of ELDEN RING."

— **Morgan Dante**, author of *PROVIDENCE GIRLS*

"Unrelenting in its descriptions and ambitious in scope, THE CRADLE OF ETERNAL NIGHT is a grim adventure that blends the visceral gut-punch of horror with the sweetness of romance, creating a tale of bittersweet hope that is as revitalizing as the dawn that follows the dark."

—**K.M. Enright**, Sunday Times Bestselling author of
MISTRESS OF LIES

"In THE CRADLE OF ETERNAL NIGHT, Ladz crafts a chilling dark fantasy that captures the bloody body horror of Bloodborne and the rotting, frozen worldbuilding of The Painted World of Ariandel. One cannot help but to root for Hanka and Basia to succeed in bringing back the light to such a cursed place."

—**Luna Fiore**, author of
WHERE WILLOWS WEEP

"An exploration of the beauty, and horror of a powerful love, THE CRADLE OF ETERNAL NIGHT is a gorgeous, sweeping, and ambitious triumph within the dark fantasy genre that seduces the reader to engage with a brutal world, versatile characters, and a romance so bittersweet and alluring that it stays with you, even when you put the book down."

—**DC Guevara** author of *A VERMILION CURSE*

"This chewable, gripping sapphic horromance has everything: monstrous lesbians, epic combat, mind-blowing lore, and decadent prose. THE CRADLE OF ETERNAL NIGHT is a triumph—perfect for anyone looking for their next dark romantasy fix."

—**Olive J. Kelley**, author of
JUNKER SEVEN

"Ladz builds worlds that are freshly unfamiliar and they never treat their audience to excessive hand holding. THE CRADLE OF ETERNAL NIGHT is fantasy for readers who are well-versed in the genre and have the fortitude to seek out the new places it can go."

—**Brent Lambert**, author of *A NECESARY CHAOS*

Also by Ladz

The Fealty of Monsters Series
Illustrated by Soren Häxan

Volume 1: The Fealty of Monsters (2024)
Volume 2: The Institute of Manners (Forthcoming)
Volume 3: Fever Dreams of Blood (Forthcoming)

Novella

Ice Upon a Pier (2023)

The Cradle of Eternal Night

Illustrated by Pom Poison

Ladz

Robot Dinosaur Press

Robot Dinosaur Press is a trademark of Chipped Cup Collective.
www.robotdinosaurpress.com

The Cradle of Eternal Night
Copyright © 2024 by Ladz.
All rights reserved.

Publication history
First Edition: October 2024

Book Cover & Interior Illustrations by Pom Poison (https://linktr.ee/pompoison)

No AI generated content was used in the creation of this book or its cover.

ISBN Data
eBook: 9798224885770
Paperback: 9798989398713

CONTENTS

Author's Note … IX

Dedication … XI

Introduction: Kolebka Wiecznej Nocy … 1

Part One: The Stars … 5

1. The Bard … 7

2. The Witch … 16

3. The Lit Road … 26

4. The Tower of the Stars … 33

Part Two: The Moons … 51

5. The Night Sky … 53

6. Old Tale … 64

7. Constructs … 86

8. Departures … 106

9. The Castle of the Twin Moons … 123

Part Three: The Sun … 141

10. The Prophet's Cathedral … 143

11. Resurrection … 157

12. The Altar of the Sun   163

13. The End   174

Glossary   181

Acknowledgments   185

About the Author   187

About the Illustrator   188

About Robot Dinosaur Press   189

Author's Note

Much like my other works, there might be some content that will be distressing, so I encourage you to read the content warnings below. Unlike my other books, there will not be a bibliography. This is a work of pure fantasy, horror, and romance, and I hope you enjoy your time in Kolebka Wiecznej Nocy.

At the end, there is a glossary featuring the place names and terms used. Most of these are terms loaned from the Polish language, and, as a native speaker, I couldn't help myself in making use of the declensions.

Content warnings

Body horror, cannibalism (both of self and others), vomiting, burning bodies, blood, gore, death of loved ones, depiction of a panic attack, trypophobia, explicit sexual content (including fingering, cunnilingus, massaging), and dubiously consensual monsterfucking

Introduction: Kolebka Wiecznej Nocy

Basia: The One Who Made It to the Kolebka

The world hasn't always been darkness.

Long ago, the Kler waged war against the technomancers, whose masterpieces of magic and engineering grew a sentience beyond simple programming and the execution of tasks. These constructs, powered by light, wreaked a havoc so great and bloody that the Kler sealed away the stars, the moons, and the sun—the Nadziemscy—from their sovereign land, the Kolebka, smothering the world in a darkness they called the Wieczna Noc.

The Kler exiled the technomancers as punishment for the crimes of their creations, commanding them to either destroy or decommission the remaining constructs. It took several generations, but the technomancers upheld their end of the bargain. In the lands beyond, constructs no longer wander free; they stay anchored to keep the artificial lights on.

The darkness, however, continues on.

OŚWIETLONA DROGA, THE LIT road, is the only light in the Kolebka not anchored to any city or town. The bright trail connects the hubs where humanity still resides, and its primary function is that of a highway for the Kler and their merchants to use. It's not for laypeople, and it's especially not for technomancers.

Basia had arrived at the Kolebka with a fellowship of twelve others who quickly learned that technomancers were not to touch its sun-embraced pavement despite it having been their ancestors who built it. Immediately alerted to their presence, the priests of the Kler had descended upon them with dark magic and sharp blades. Only half the group survived that encounter. The rest of them fell one by one to the night-kissed beasts and the roving priests.

They're all gone now, and Basia races alone alongside the grand, brilliant highway. She thought it would be her and Mirek making their way to Tawerna, a town very close to one of the chapels where the Kler sealed away the lights, the Nadziemskie Kaplice: the tower of stars, Gwiedzna Wieża. His screams follow her instead.

No matter how hard she pumps her arms and lifts her legs along the snowbank tucked away from the Oświetlona Droga where the stone glows with white light, Tawerna, the enormous residence shining through the darkness like a beacon, grows no closer.

She doesn't stop running until the snapping jaws and clicking chitin of the night-kissed beasts grow fainter, until she's certain they have lost interest in following her. Exhausted by her flight and giving in to grief, Basia collapses forward into the frost. Her sword falls from her hands as she braces her fall. The ground's coolness soothes the anger gathering in her eyes and cheeks. Its cold sting almost staunches the tears but fails.

She doesn't want to be left alone in these forbidden lands. She had never been exceptional, and no one counted on her to survive in any skirmish. Her gift is her cleverness which more often than not preserved only herself with no regard for others. She had been chastised for it, but that selfishness helped her make it this far into the Kolebka. Poor Mirek told her to run, so she did. There were no second chances for him, not with his spent resurrection stone, and Basia had saved hers for herself, not that she can administer it on herself now she's alone.

There are no technomancers in Kolebka Wiecznej Nocy. The Kler made sure of that.

Basia rolls over onto her large backpack and stares at the black, vacant sky above. The ceaseless darkness no longer instills a bone-deep fear. When she first came to the Kolebka it felt like a great maw, ready to swallow her whole. Having been in the Kolebka's wilderness long enough for the sight to grow familiar, however, she knows it's the Kler she should be afraid of, but it's the kind of fear that fuels a fight, rather than fleeing to safer shores. Nowhere is safe for her here, especially as the Kler likely has a presence in every enclave. Even Tawerna.

All she needs is to get inside undetected, assuming the Kler is not in the process of strengthening the darkness in case any technomancers still roam the Kolebka. The laity doesn't know the Wieczna Noc is an oppression crafted by magic, not a natural disaster. She hates having to shoulder the responsibility of dispelling the lie on her own. Generations of lies will be crashing down under the weight of her sword.

She slides out from within her bag's straps, undoes the tie, and searches for her notebook. The fellowship's notes are incomplete, but it's enough to get to Tawerna. From there, she can get the directions to Gwiedzna Wieża. It cannot be far off, but she knows the Kler can't have made it easy to find one of their holy sites. It can't help that Basia has never had a talent for finding things, either. She's spent so much time with the texts that these notes appear behind her eyes when she shuts them. If the notes are right, Tawerna will have the missing details somewhere within the Mistrz's studies and offices. She doesn't doubt that the Kler will be there to receive her.

What she knows of the priests is that they never intended to bring the light back. They have never acted of the goodness of their own hearts; it's time someone demanded answers and undid their perpetual reign. All things must come to an end, and that includes this night, even if it has already cost her a dozen people she considered friends and comrades, claimed by the Kler's magic or the sharp claws of their beasts roaming these darkened lands.

As much as she fears fighting the Kler and their Strażnicy guards all by herself, she knows it won't be where her life ends. She is determined to die to the violence of something worse than the night-kissed beasts that have been hunting her since her fellowship arrived in the Kolebka, something awakened by the sun's oppressive rays.

PART ONE: THE STARS

CHAPTER ONE

THE BARD

MIREK: THE NOBLE FOOL WHOSE HEART HAD NO PLACE IN THE OUTSIDE

IN THE TOWN CALLED Tawerna, its bard, Hanka, sits atop the banquet hall's rafters and drops a lively ditty on the diners' heads below. It is a feast like she has never seen.

At the center of the titanic central table lays a glistening swine much larger than the beasts typically served at dinner. In a wreath around it are several heaps of crisped potatoes, drowning in a pool of gravy dolloped elegantly with jam and cream. The crunching of crisp, fresh breads mingles among the idle conversations. The enticing smells give her some trouble with the words and the tune falling out of her mouth. It's a complicated piece, and a fitting finale to her tenure as one of Tawerna's many singers and musicians. She might be missed, but she hopes they'll forget about her as the final note leaves her lips.

Hanka hops off her perch. As much as the rumbling in her stomach wants her to partake and indulge, this meal isn't for her.

The feast honors the visiting Kler, the world's aloof caretakers. From their bastion in Katedra Wieszczów, they worship and wait for an eventual return of light to this realm swallowed in darkness. They sing praises to the Nadziemscy—the sun, the moons, and the stars which no one in Kolebka Wiecznej Nocy and the lands beyond have seen in generations. They beg. They pray. They encourage others to beg and pray.

What the Kler hasn't told anyone is this: it is entirely up to them whether the light returns or not.

Hanka was never supposed to find out—her own reckless curiosity led her to it. Afterward, she had escaped Katedra Wieszczów, making her way into Tawerna around when the Kler last visited on a pilgrimage to Gwiedzna Wieża, which she also wasn't supposed to know about. Their paths hadn't crossed then. She wonders why they're crossing now. *If* they're crossing now; she can't tell if she's what they seek. It's likely. It's an encounter she's been waiting for since she arrived. Thus, she needs to leave before they discover her presence. It's a matter of when, not if.

In addition to the feast and the excitement, there are other signs of their visitation. Night's kiss—a miasma dark and unseen by those who cannot wield it—pools around their feet, trailing behind them like a veil. They dress in uniforms: funereal black hoods with white, collared surcoats of different cuts and shapes. Some wear black skirts, others black trousers, while others parade around in just black smallclothes and tall socks. Silvers chains and belts keep the articles of clothing from falling off their frames, while the silver eye-shaped pendants on each torso tells the world that they are the vigilant Kler. Despite the Kolebka's ceaseless darkness, they protect their eyes with charcoal gray bands so as not to be blinded by the celestials they worship so fervently.

She had removed hers when she left the Katedra. Her eyes afforded her special vision within the darkness, though she had worried that the Mistrz of Tawerna would report her to the Kler upon her arrival. He hadn't; there was too much pity. Lone wanderers were upsettingly common—night-kiss beasts often attacked those who traveled along Oświetlona Droga. Tawerna's ministry took her in exchange for her musical services, and she performed well enough to be hired. Her continued musicianship allowed her to blend in with the others. No one questioned her slit pupils or bright blue eyes. No one suspected she wasn't human.

There is only one person who knows that truth about Hanka, and he eats with Tawerna's Mistrz on the opposite end of the hall along with four other priests. Pale yellow hair swoops across the left half his face like a crescent moon. Though his eyes are obscured by his own band, she knows he shares her cerulean irises. She recalls him wanting jewelry threaded into his skin, and it glints now in the banquet hall's many torches. A ring in his lip connects by a chain to the ring on his ear on his left side. Another ring graces his brow—she hadn't expected that one. In the time since they had last seen each other, his face has only grown more severe, cheeks and chin sharpening, but she recognizes him by demeanor and posture.

Patryk was her broodmate. Both of them are night-kissed beasts who were born to masquerade as human.

Should she have stayed with him to become a priest herself? Probably. But Patryk had aided her escape, neither of them knowing what would happen if the Kler found out that a creature they had made knew their truth. It's his presence that now convinces her that this pilgrimage is definitely to retrieve her, to take her back to Katedra Wieszczów. For punishment or execution, she doesn't know.

As she turns to leave, one of the bards calls to her. "Oi, Hanka!" She hopes he didn't just expose her to Patryk.

It's never been important to know all the other bards by name; if she guessed Jan, she would have a significant chance of guessing correctly. She closes her eyes and gives him a smile. "That was a wonderful performance you gave earlier, Jan."

He doesn't correct her on his name. "Thank you! I have a message from the Mistrz on behalf of the Kler to share with you, if you've got a moment."

She swallows. She does not have a moment, but a message from the Mistrz might be worth taking one. "Let's have it."

Jan leans in, smelling sharply of samogon and pepper, and whispers into her ear, "There is a technomancer in Tawerna. They're telling us to keep an eye out."

This catches Hanka by surprise. She's not human, but she's no technomancer. They had been long exiled from the Kolebka at the behest of the Kler. It happened during the Zaćmienie—the event which sealed away the stars, the moons, and the sun—long before Hanka spawned. "I'll keep an eye out."

She will not. She has somewhere else to be, anywhere but Tawerna.

She politely bids him a good rest and puts her focus into hiding her haste. She briefly debates leaving her balalaika behind in the feasting hall, not even bringing it back to her room—it likely won't survive another journey through the night. Though it's a technomancer artifact that the Kler clearly didn't mind her stealing, too many years have passed since she last cast a spell with it. Perhaps the little bulb at the top of its neck no longer works. She decides to keep it regardless—the next town might need a bard, and she will happily take on the role again. The instrument will be a boon, not be a burden.

Jan makes no motion to beg her to stay for the feast; she will not be missed. She has rarely paid attention to when other bards do or don't eat with the rest of Tawerna at the communal meal. She doesn't want to be there when the Kler sits among the dining citizens. She wants nothing to do with the fact that the Kler hunts a technomancer, even though it means they're not hunting her.

Ignoring the scarceness of Tawerna's halls—the entire population of the single-building town is at the feast—Hanka makes it back to her room. It suddenly feels as new as when she first arrived. Her pack sits where it had been this whole time; she never unpacked. It made her sad to keep her scant belongings in a large backpack, aside from the new acquisitions which she kept in drawers, but at any time, the Kler could arrive and usher a swift departure. Tawerna had never felt like home to her, only a pause before the nebulous next escape, but it felt more welcoming and familiar than Katedra Wieszczów ever had.

Here, she had a routine, some familiarity.

Here, none of the people scared her.

Here, she kept no one else's secrets nor offered any information unsolicited. As long as she plucked at her balalaika in turn and in lockstep with the musicians around her, no one suspected a beast among them.

She goes through the belongings she acquired here—wood carvings and other small trinkets. Some of the crude jewelry had never been worn. She's going to leave these petty treasures behind. Money has long been meaningless in these night-bound lands and the only currency comes in the form of service. Music is an endless well in that way, unless someone outright refuses it. Hasn't happened yet. She will count that blessing.

She counts, too, the blessing that she has kept her blond tresses clipped short; she will not get burrs trapped in in it, as she did on her first escape.

There isn't much in her sack. A few changes of clothes, her own journals and other notes she had stolen from the Katedra. There's an exit through the pantry, so she can nick provisions on her way out. No one would be there during the feast—it's the best exit. Once that food runs out, she'll manage. She foraged well enough in the Kolebka's woods and plains before, despite having only her own night vision to guide her way. If her freedom and survival are to be assured, the land will provide. Otherwise, perhaps her liberty from the Kler and its teachings is not meant to be. She's had a good run.

Hanka strips out of her self-assigned bard's uniform, peeling off the linen tunic and wool trousers. She needs more layers where she's going. The last season the world saw before the Wieczna Noc was winter and, because the sun's rays had never reappeared long enough to melt the snow, the snow remained. The only flora and fauna living wild in these lands are those which can survive such conditions—agriculture has retreated into greenhouses built from the scraps and engines of abandoned technomancer constructs. Tawerna has several such feats of engineering and technology. Were she to look out, their dimmed lights glow softly white just beyond the wall separating them from the courtyard leading back to the central residential keep.

She'll need to make it down to that courtyard: it's the final space between Tawerna and the world beyond. It doesn't lead to the Droga, but no one has ever had trouble finding that shimmering, glowing gravel road snaking through the Kolebka.

Knocks come to her door. She swallows as she slowly puts on a chemise to preserve some of her modesty. The soft fabric hangs loosely off her body as it settles around on her round hips and soft stomach. She never expects visitors—if she wanted company during sleeping hours, it had always been her making the visitation.

Knocks come again. If it's the Kler, they found a way to suppress their miasma and replace it with the radiant golden glow that sneaks in under the threshold. That glow reminds her of the captured technomancer in the Katedra who taught her how to play the balalaika and gifted her the instrument. They had taken pity on Hanka, the inquisitive beast, and slaked their own loneliness by inviting her into their cell. They had been like Hanka, kindred spirits kept from the rest of the Katedra, until the Kler could no longer deny that both Hanka and Patryk had more in common with humanity that the night-kissed, even while her friend had remained alone.

Perhaps the technomancer the Kler hunts is Hanka's old friend. There wouldn't be another one in the Kolebka. If there had been, why would they expose their magic like that? If Hanka can see it, the priests of the Kler can too, which puts this visitor in danger.

The knocks come one more time. Hanka opens the door. The woman on the other side barrels inside, gesturing for Hanka to close it.

"Can I help you?" Hanka's voice is as small as the thud which shuts the door. No one has ever forced an entry like that.

"The Kler is after me." The woman pants after every word. She throws off the one-strapped leather sack hanging off her shoulder. It hits the floor with a thump.

Hanka sees the aura that glows off her pale skin and knows immediately that she lacks night's kiss; this woman is not human. Impossibly, she's the second technomancer Hanka has ever met. These sun-embraced witches once manipulated light with magic, creating constructs whose defunct chassis and hollowed-out corpses now keep Kolebskie towns operational. She knew they weren't a myth, but neither did she think she would meet another one in her lifetime.

But unlike how Hanka pictures a legend, this technomancer is Hanka's own diminutive stature. Her midnight-black hair hangs from her head in a full, thick tail, with long pieces framing her face. A large, curved sword wrapped with thorned wire sits against her back. Its tip almost scratches the floor as the technomancer straightens. Charms in different triangular and spherical shapes dangle from its fat hilt. There are other smaller decorations on the two daggers hanging from the belt on her waist. They sparkle in the lantern light, but Hanka doesn't focus on them. She looks at the metal plates protecting the witch's knuckles and fingers. They're threaded into thick black wool that climbs up her arms. A band of flesh peeks out from beneath the belt wrapped around her thick bicep. Her ebony shirt has no sleeves and covers her stomach.

Another flat piece of leather with bulges like pockets protects her chest, smoothing her bosom but not flattening it.

Hanka blushes at the exposed flesh from where her top connects at her crotch and the way her sable skirt hangs askew with its golden needles, showing off her hip. Hanka cannot even begin to guess what weighs her pockets down so much. Her large, black boots shine with melted snow.

"Now, why would the Kler be after you?" Hanka says. Her hands hang at her sides. She doesn't know if she can touch this intruder. She doesn't how, or if, she should help.

"I'm not supposed to be here. Not in Tawerna, but *here*." She gestures to show the floor around her. "I just needed somewhere to hide from the beasts for a bit, and, well, *they* found me."

"I see." Hanka doesn't know if she should mention that she isn't supposed to be in Tawerna either. "You picked the wrong door, I'm afraid. I'm actually on my way out."

"You're joking." The witch raises a thick brow, glancing at Hanka's scant belongings. "What could a bard possibly have done to also be on the run from the Kler?"

"I'm sorry, I don't think you get to ask questions." She inhales and crosses her arms. She still has so much packing to do. "What's in the bag?" It's twice the size of Hanka's. If the bard had to guess, this technomancer had left on the long journey to the Kolebka prepared to wander these darkened lands a very long time.

The visitor, seemingly unbothered, undoes the thick knot keeping the leather straps in place. With a muffled pop, the lid opens. In the harsh shadows of her bedroom, she cannot see the inside.

A notebook comes out first. It bulges from its stitching. The technomancer's fingers flip through it, landing on a page with an illustration that reminds Hanka of the regional maps she had seen during her time in the Katedra. "Do you know of a tower nearby?"

Gwiedzna Wieża. "I do."

"I'll protect you if you lead me to it."

"I don't recall offering to lead you there." Gwiedzna Wieża is one of three holy places in the Kolebka. The Kler controls who wanders the roads and who can enter those sacred spaces, which most of the laypeople don't even know about. But Hanka does. "What does a technomancer want with the Wieża anyway?"

"The Kler is hiding something, and I intend to find out what it is." Her visitor rises and wraps her palm around her hilt. "Unless you know what's in there."

Hanka has other things to do than get murdered by an intruder, so she might as well give a morsel of truth. "I might. And I can guide you there. If you'll protect me." It'll mean leaving for one of the last places Hanka expects the Kler to find her.

The technomancer narrows her deep brown eyes at Hanka. "Are you that eager to leave?"

"Perhaps."

"And how can I trust that you won't turn me in as soon as we abandon this room?"

Hanka says the most honest thing she knows. "I don't believe their lies either."

The technomancer's dark brown eyes blink wide open. The way her pink lips part, however, suggest pleasant surprise. Like relief.

She places her gloved hands on Hanka's cheeks and pulls her close, kissing her. Hanka gasps, if only because she didn't expect such tender thanks. This woman isn't the enemy—at least, she's no friend of the Kler. Neither is Hanka. Perhaps a partnership can be born of that shared distrust.

What also delights Hanka is her warmth. The world outside Tawerna's walls is vast, quiet, dark, and cold. Hanka places her hands on the technomancer's hips and feels heat radiating against her hands. Both their hearts sound loud to Hanka's ears.

Before Hanka has a chance for her tongue to get a taste of this intruder, she pulls away and says, "I promise we can continue this later, but first, we must leave."

The technomancer nods. "I'll remember that." She lets go of Hanka, who goes back to packing.

Her lips still tingle and a giddiness dances at the base of her throat. The last time she left, she had been alone. It will be nice to have someone with whom to wander the Kolebka for a bit.

As she collects the clothes from the bottom of her dresser, Hanka remembers how good she had it in Tawerna: the anonymity, the good meals, the art. The Kler kept their distance, likely because Tawerna's good nature served a purpose: to keep people jolly and disinterested in the world beyond. It helped them ignore the truth of the outside with its parks, courtyards, and greenhouses. The warmth and noise of the indoors obfuscated the frigid silence of the beyond.

An abyss which Hanka will no longer have to traverse alone.

CHAPTER TWO

THE WITCH

THE PILGRIM: WE NEVER LEARNED THEIR NAME

THIS DIVERSION IS WORKING out better than expected. Instead of meeting violence, Basia opened a door and met a companion perhaps more valuable than the dozen who died getting Basia to Tawerna. This one somehow knows about the Kler's deception. On their way to the Gwiedzna Wieża, Basia can ask more of what she knows.

It's not just this knowledge that intrigues Basia about her host, but also that someone else might also be the Kler's target. She's so desperate to leave, but she's no technomancer. Though they don't share any one look, Basia knew all the technomancers returning to the Kolebka, saw them all die. She knows what a technomancer aura looks like. Nothing shines off the bard, not the technomancer's white golden corona nor the billowing cascade of darkness that follows the Kler's steps. She seems to Basia to be another layperson, and what manner of punishment would the Kler have to dole out to the people they sealed the stars, moons, and sun from? Isn't the ceaseless dark harm enough?

She watches the bard pack, rolling up some shirts and trousers into neat bundles with belts, socks, and smallclothes. It seems she's been a marauder for quite some time—it's hypnotic to watch her elegant, string-roughed hands work so intricately with fibers that had likely been woven to withstand the weather beyond.

It's what the bard isn't packing that catches Basia's full attention. "Are you not bringing any weapons?"

The bard looks up. Basia doesn't know what to make of her eyes. The slit suggests they're like an animal's, primed for living in the dark, not the rounded pupils of someone human.

"I've never had a need of them," she responds.

"If you say so." Basia then looks down her own chest at her crossed arms while the bard puts on additional layers. It's the smallest amount of privacy that can be afforded.

She doesn't know how much time and quiet passes when the bard finally says, "You can look up now."

The clothing she wears will do well in the snows beyond. She wears a thick coat gray like stained silver. A white scarf with a pattern of large black squares surrounds her neck—its ends connect in a perfect circle, unlike the twin tails Basia has seen from other places. A black hat hangs slouched off the bard's head. Her black leather gloves lack fingertips, leaving her callused pads vulnerable to the elements. Bunched up socks provide insulation where her pants end. Though her boots stop at her ankles, the soles look well-worn and heavy—the slippers that previously graced her feet lay beside the bed. A memento of her life here.

Her smaller backpack hangs off both her shoulders. Where Basia would affix a weapon, either the belt of a scabbard crossing her chest or on her shoulders, the bard carries her instrument. How will that be helpful? Perhaps it is precious to her, but such delicacy will only endanger the both of them.

Basia never previously questioned or instructed her other companions on what they could or could not carry—it might have been their downfall. The fellowship didn't give much instruction, but Basia wants to survive long enough to see the end, so all the items and effects Basia wields are or can be made useful. Even her notebooks with all the information there is to know about her journey can be burned for warmth or visibility in a pinch.

Despite knowing better as a result of the trail of corpses in her wake, Basia can't bring herself to tell the bard that perhaps she should leave the instrument behind. For all she knows, it might hold the kind of significance that warrants its presence almost like a third companion. Basia has not yet been able to discard the remembrances of her fallen fellowship. It would be hypocritical to demand someone leave behind a tool that satisfies a need other than survival.

"Are you sure you have everything?" Basia sees countless things scattered throughout the room: clothes not quite suited for long journeys, baubles and jewelry, likely gifts from the patrons of Tawerna. Things that hold no meaning in the slumbering world, where the currency is favors exchanged and jobs performed. There might be treasures preserved from the time before the Wieczna Noc that could be worth something, but if Basia thought like the Kler, she'd want it all hidden away or destroyed.

How dare there be evidence of a world different than the murk they all inhabit.

The bard purses her lips and spins around, doing one more glance around her space. "I'd say so. Anything else can be found elsewhere."

Basia nods, trying to quiet the discomfort that says something is missing. The feeling tells her nothing specific, but it still refuses to be easily quelled.

"I suggest we exit via the pantry," the bard says as she crosses her room. "We can nick some treats for the road."

"Treats?"

"I think staying well-fed is important. Keeps the mind sharp and the senses awake."

Basia has never valued comforts—the roots and the meat provided by the wilderness have kept her fed enough. What little food has comforted her on this journey were pickled vegetables she stole from her family's home before leaving. She didn't say good-bye and never apologized, but the empty vessels have made for great flasks in which she can melt the ever-present snow when thirsty. "Won't there be anyone in the pantry during a feast?"

The bard shakes her head. "The people here mostly keep to themselves. If there's anyone around, they won't do anything. Most of the laypeople can't see magic anyway. Trust me, I wouldn't have lasted here as long as I have if people had been curious."

Basia has never lived in a town like this one. She doesn't know what's considered normal or what a routine is. She trained to hunt constructs, her life measured by the whims and needs of the hunt. Sometimes, before coming to the Kolebka, she would visit the little worlds behind walls illuminated by technomantic tricks and tools, but not long enough to know that stability. The bard seems open to sharing that knowledge, so Basia keeps her protests deep within her chest.

The bard opens the door and allows Basia to exit first. When the door clicks closed, the bard doesn't bother locking it. Instead, she leads them down the carpeted hallway. Asking out loud if the bard is sure they're going the right way would invite suspicion. Basia's lips remain tightly shut.

Instead of guiding them to the angular, spiraling staircase that Basia climbed earlier, the bard opens an unassuming brown door between two entrances that must lead to other flats. This one leads to a shaft which holds up a very tall ladder.

As if anticipating Basia's question, the bard says, "It's how staff get around Tawerna without being noticed." Basia isn't surprised; her face never fails to reveal her true feelings, even if they're mostly confusion and exhaustion.

The bard adjusts her instrument, making sure it points behind her as she puts a foot on the first rung. "I'll meet you at the bottom."

A swish of leather gliding against metal follows her as she descends. Basia leans forward over the edge. Despite the lights, she can barely make out the bottom. What a strange way to travel.

She grips the bars and takes a deep breath. If the woman who's lived in relative comfort can slide so easily, so can Basia. When she lets go, the metal of the ladder whistles under the fabric of her gloves sliding over it. The drop and steady descent send her guts to the base of her throat. A scream will do more harm than good, and if she thinks about it too much, the scant contents of her stomach will wind up on the wrong side of her body. It scares her, this speed. The tension between a body and the ground should not be so deadly.

The echoes get closer, suggesting that bottom rapidly approaches. Trying not to think about the potential injuries, she squeezes the bars of the ladder tightly, putting as much force into her knuckles and fingers as she can muster. The whistling escalates into a whine as she slows down, but not enough to stop the way her feet land hard and her knees bend sharply under the weight of her sword and her pack. She reaches into one of the pockets of her chest piece to pull out a tab of poppy to chew on. The pain eases immediately. It's not something she relies on often—she has plenty to spare—but it's preventative; she needs to be able to run as soon as they leave Tawerna.

Pain relieved, Basia searches the small room she's landed in to find the bard in the act of popping open the door to the pantry. It is a dank, small space. Not deep enough to be a cellar, although the stale air caught among the uneven shelves overflowing with dry goods begs to differ. Smaller lights dot the walls, which turn on upon their entrance. The bard goes over to several of the half-open sacks and starts taking. Basia stands back, unsure what manner of meal can be scavenged from a place like this. All she sees are ingredients, but if the bard is openly offering her expertise of these enclaves and storage spaces, Basia will make the most of it.

The bard sets her backpack on the floor, undoing the knot keeping it steady to shove several sachets inside. Basia can't tell the contents from the smells—she stands too far back.

Pleased with her work, the bard says, "This should be enough provisions until we get to another town."

Basia knows better than to shout her incredulity about going to another town, even if, with how little she knows of the location to the two other Nadziemskie Strażnicy, it will be necessary to stop and explore other archives.

For all their haste, she has to ask, "Before we leave, I need to go to the Tawerna archives."

The bard widens her eyes at Basia. "The Mistrz is probably still eating, and I am not going to bring more attention to myself with a break-in."

From the fellowship's notes, Basia knows the Mistrzowie of the towns are appointed by the Kler to rule and keep the peace. That includes ensuring no one gets into the archives, that they keep the truth of the darkness just out of sight and out of mind for the people living within it. Instead of destroying that knowledge, they scattered it throughout the Kolebka, safely out of the reach of troublesome technomancers seeking to undo their work.

"I know about the Wieża, anyway," the bard adds. "I don't think the Mistrzowie do, and I'm not about to find out."

It seems doubtful, but she has to ask. "And how do I know that you're not the Mistrz?"

The bard raises an eyebrow. "I'm not sure they are allowed to break their rituals, not even in emergencies."

"Emergencies?"

"Five Kler visiting Tawerna in search of not one but two trespassers? I'd call that an emergency." So far, the bard seems so much like any other layperson. Nothing about her disposition or presence suggests that she might endanger the Kler or their congregation at any point. She seems harmless and tame—no one dangerous asks for protection in exchange of services.

Basia grunts in response. "You have a point."

"Speaking of, I have what I need and then some more for you too. Come on, let's leave." She puts her pack back on, then the instrument. It hangs at her side awkwardly, but her movements suggest she's used to traveling with it the way Basia carries her sword.

The bard leads them to a wall with a faint outline. She manipulates the latch and pushes. It's not enough force. They push together against the thick pantry exit. Judging by the way it shrieks and scrapes against its hinges, it never gets much action. It seems foolish to Basia to use such cacophony as their means of escape, but she doesn't have any better ideas. The only other option would be to fight the residents of Tawerna, and such a waste of energy and blood would only get in her way.

Once upon a time, she did not immediately see violence as the only option. Those days are long gone—that penchant for peace might have died with the penultimate member of the fellowship. Since then, she's been alone, not able to trust any other traveler she's come across.

This bard, however—this one she might keep around. If she knows of Gwiedzna Wieża, perhaps she knows the Kler's other secrets.

Hanka goes first, guiding the two of them across the courtyard. Large braziers contain fires dancing in orange, yellow, and white, cheap imitations of the great celestial lights which once leaped across the sky. Basia has only heard stories. She's going to make it real.

"You there, halt!"

They should have continued, but they both halt, turning to follow the voice's direction. Five members of the Kler stand beneath the awning to the general entrance to the banquet hall. Behind the frosted window are shifting lights and shadow as the people inside cannot at all fathom the blood to be shed. Do they even know of death and loss?

Basia grasps the hilt of her sword, twisting to free it from the lock that allows it to hang on her back. She draws an arc around her head, her charms passing in front of her mouth. She whispers the spell to imbue them with star fire. It bursts down the length of her sword, the rivulets glowing brilliant white. It shines like a torch.

"I halted. What do you want?" Basia barks at them.

The middle priest speaks first. "To stay. To join us for the feast." The invitation sounds gentle, sounds human. It mostly sounds like a trap.

She cannot read the faces obscured by their hooded veils and eye bands. All the lights show are their chins, some bare and others with beards thick as the pelts of the night-kissed beasts that wander the Kolebka's wilderness. Like the night-kissed beasts these sorcerers *are*. She's taken them down before; she'll eliminate them again.

"Hanka, please," the priest on the far left says. "Come with us."

Of the group, he is the most bare. While the others wear their ivory brooches close to their necks or high on their chests, this one wears it like a buckle around his waist. His hood's fabric panels are tucked into the belt, loose and billowing like the way his skirt-like trousers tuck into his silver-tipped slippers. She sees every gray scar on his chest matted with hair the same white as the hair on his head. His bareness is a dare. It's an *invitation*.

His left hand grips an obsidian staff threaded with silver, atop which sits a spherical cage trapping dark blue gems. On his right hand he wears a heavy glove which reminds Basia of the technomancers who fight with their fists rather than with swords or axes, like those companions the priests took from her. She wonders if he now carries their weapons as trophies.

As much as she would like to sink her blade into every sorcerer before her, it would do nothing but get in the way of her finding the first of many slivers of truth about this world's darkness. She also has a bard to protect. If there's any hope of "continuing later," Basia needs to keep her out of harm's way. She needs to get them both away from the Kler.

Basia's fingers curl around the charm named wyjaśnić. She blows onto its smooth glass. The flame around her sword bursts into an inferno.

"Run, Hanka." The name falls awkwardly off Basia's lips because that's what the priest called her; the bard should have offered it herself willingly.

Instead of dashing off as commanded, Hanka takes a few steps backward, not wanting to vanish from the courtyard. Is she that worried about losing sight of Basia? If Hanka were so scared of the wilderness, why didn't she get weapons? They cannot be so hard to procure.

Basia ignores her doubts and takes a step forward, slashing her sword in a wide, horizontal arc. It leaves a flare behind it, scorching the stone ground. The priests cast their magic. Its cool, glowing spray turns into thick mist. She slashes again and again. They extinguish her sunlit flame and launch their brackish waves back at her. Whiteness enshrouds them—a perfect cover.

Their fighting prowess surprises Basia. In all her time in the Kolebka, not once has Basia directly crossed blades or magic with a priest. She's either killed them before they noticed her or she did not come close to them at all. But outdoors, they usually wander in pairs. To see five together? They must need more power to complete their task. But glancing at Hanka, Basia sees no threat. She's willowy and soft, gentle, even.

Of the two of them, only Basia looks like an emergency. Armed with forbidden magic and her sword, she is dangerous.

Hanka takes her balalaika and holds it against her stomach. The instrument cannot be a weapon; it's not something the technomancers worked on. Laypeople can't have augmented it, so it's likely Kler wizardry. But then Basia's gaze catches on the small glass knob at the top of the instrument and she cannot believe her eyes—it's the same kind of trinket as the charms hanging off her sword. The torrent of questions gets lodged in her throat while she hears a familiar spell come out of Hanka's lips.

"Rozpalić," she says, voice even. It's as if she doesn't want to use her mouth for violence.

If only Basia had ever been allowed to be so tender and pleasant.

Hanka pinches her fingers together and strums against the instrument's three strings. They ring out, dingling in that way the instrument's tones do. A great flame crafted from the sun's embrace much like her sword's bursts forth in a sweeping arch. It catches the priests off guard to be fighting two technomancers, but not enough to lower their defenses. Not enough to see themselves out and let the two of them go.

The one who knew Hanka's name douses himself in that sodden sorcery, powering through the fire in a mass of mist. Hanka unleashes more flames, her song playing louder and louder, taking large steps backwards with each chord and progression. Basia slashes her blade at the same rhythm, creating a rolling wave of destructive light. It only creates more fog, blocking their vision.

Whiteness as thick as the darkness swallows them all. The ringing notes are the loudest, followed by the grunts of Kler struggling to douse the flames. They're wasting time and energy on this. Basia diminishes the flame around her weapon and cuts a path through the fog. The only way she knows where Hanka stands is the sound of her instrument. But the music stops suddenly and a hand grabs Basia's wrist.

Hanka pulls them both out into a clearer section of the courtyard, towards the gate leading not to the Droga but to the sable wilderness beyond.

"What about them?" Basia asks, worried that the Kler will follow them. If it would be worth the effort, she'd try to slaughter them—they've taken so much from her already. But it might not be, and the uncertainty proves a burden.

Hanka doesn't answer with words. Instead, she tweaks the knob at the top of her balalaika and exhales. On the inhale, she plays a horrible tune, one more in harmony with the screeches of the night-kissed beasts than any ditty or walking song Basia ever heard.

She tries not to shriek when large, furred masses of shadows leap into the courtyard from the woods outside. Even in the lights, she cannot make out their shapes—their flesh swallows the scant light. The night-kissed beasts ignore Basia, racing past them much to her relief. Hanka doesn't let her gaze at them long. She pulls Basia behind.

The sounds following their escape are the gnashing of jaws, the drumming of shell against shell, and panicked screams of beings Basia didn't think could ever experience fear.

CHAPTER THREE

THE LIT ROAD

VASILISA: WHO DIED OF EXPOSURE

HANKA'S EYES WORK ABOUT as well in the dark as those of her kin. Humans allegedly only see darkness as if their eyes are mirrors to the world's shadows. The night-kissed beasts, however, see a world veiled in gray. In the woods outside of Tawerna, sturdy tree trunks rise from the snow-covered ground. Not a small critter makes itself known, though Hanka would be able to see their shapes clearly among the drift.

It's how she knows where to run while dragging Basia along by the wrist. They didn't stop long enough for her to put away her balalaika or for the technomancer to put away her sword or to rearrange her backpack against her shoulder. Hanka didn't want them to get lost among teeth and claws or further ensnared in the fog. If some of the flames missed the Kler and set fire to Tawerna, it wouldn't be the worst of the terrible hosting gifts she left behind.

Hanka dreams of a day when she can apologize for the destruction that follows in her wake.

Throughout the Kolebka along the myriad paths branching from the Droga are sheds like abandoned homes where the Kler resupplies when moving between their sacred sites. The reason one lies so close to Tawerna is this: the path to Gwiedzna Wieża is too vertical and too narrow to build any other kind of structure, their location too secret to be accessible to the laity.

Through the dark, she sees the night-kissed edges of the dilapidated shack that serves as a rest stop for priests making pilgrimage. The two of them should be safe there for as long as the beasts keep the priests occupied. Hanka isn't sure if the priests have it in them to destroy their own creations. Even during that final encounter in Katedra Wieszczów, they should have made her regret being spawned, not allowed her to run away. She doesn't think it was out of mercy. If the true reason is hers to know, she will learn it eventually.

"Wait here," Hanka says, lying about the distance to the hovel's door. She can barely make out its shape—the technomancer cannot see it at all.

She gets up on her toes and takes long, leaping steps. For a human, she's small, but for a beast, even more so. She lands soundlessly, though she worries that the witch might have a piece of technology that enables preternatural hearing. Or, if technomancers aren't human in the same way the night-kissed beasts and the Kler are, their ears are just wired to hear more than they should because of magic or biological manipulation. It's a foolish thing to worry about.

Her hand finds the knob's stinging cold metal. She tries to turn it. Nothing. The old locks are in place. They can only be undone by night-kissed magic. Magic like what Hanka has; what Hanka *is*.

The witch knows what the priest's sorcery looks like. After having seen the scant technomancy Hanka had stolen from Katedra Wieszczów, Basia cannot find out that Hanka knows both types of magic. Not this soon, anyway.

Hanka inhales, reaching inside herself to find the current, those dark waters threaded with reflected moonlight. It's shallow—she hasn't consumed night-kissed flesh in some time—but it's there, like the last blemish of a puddle after a storm. The magic catches, swimming up to her shoulder and sluicing down to her hand. It beads upon her fingers and melts into the knob's grooves.

It's enough. The door clicks open.

"Is everything all right?" the technomancer shouts.

Things have never been more fine. "I got the door open!" Hanka takes the same leaps back to the technomancer, who hasn't moved except to adjust her belongings.

"Door? What door are you talking about? Are we at the Wieża?"

"Not quite." Hanka makes sure not to sound like she had exerted herself, despite the way her lungs heave and the dizziness fills her head. It's silly—the technomancer will soon see how far the rest stop is from where Hanka asked her to wait. She needs to come up with an excuse. "The Kler needs places of respite too. Get their bearings together before making it to the Wieża, you know. It's a long trek."

"Is this a trap? How do you know the Kler isn't waiting to ambush us?"

Hanka can't say it's because she cannot sense them. Their night-kissed magic calls to her like a master whistling for their hound. "The door was wide open and there's no one inside." She shrugs and gives the technomancer a smile she can't see.

The witch clicks her tongue. "I have to believe you, then, don't I?"

"I don't think so, actually." Hanka's face shudders, the muscles contracting and blinking her eyes closed. The kin she summoned for their escape are dead or dying. The Kler might be winning—the two of them don't have long to dawdle. They cannot stay here long.

"What." The word is more a bark than a statement.

"If you would like to unpack out here in the wilderness, that's on you. I'm going inside to figure out where I'm going next." Hanka turns around and makes her footfalls heavy, playful, and petulant, crunching loudly against the snow.

"You said you'd guide me."

"Only if you protect me. It's hard to do that if we separate." Hanka knows she's being dramatic, but the pain from the night-kissed beasts' brawling with the Kler keeps knocking into her like waves against a shore.

All she can hope for is that the Kler leaves the two of them to die in the wilderness—it's what they do to all wanderers who choose not to use the Droga. The Kler abandons them to their fate. It's not their job to protect those who eschew their divine protection.

Hanka doesn't glance to see if the technomancer follows her. She listens to her footfalls sinking into the snowpack, struggling beneath the weight of a sword and a too-big sack.

"How far is it?" the witch calls.

"Just a few more paces. I'll catch you if you trip."

She means it more in jest—the witch is more than careful and capable, despite her momentary struggle. She must have been out in the darkness for a long time to need so many provisions. She's decent with a sword, though she lacks experience going hand-to-hand with the Kler. They exiled the technomancers; they're the ones who made an art out of fighting the sun-embraced.

No one in the Kolebka would have been able to teach her either. As far as Hanka knows, none of the laypeople have ever revolted; none of them would be a font of that knowledge. As far as anyone living in the Kolebka knows, peace rules these tenebrous lands. There is no conflict just as there is no light. The only differences lie in who can and cannot manipulate magic.

Being night-kissed like the Kler is a vocation as much as it is a blessing of supernatural abilities. It's a job and a responsibility Hanka wants no part of. Her escape is a transgression against the agreement that had been her birth. A vow broken, and there still have been no consequences.

Hanka opens the door and searches for anything resembling a light switch. She should have thought to activate the lights before the technomancer followed her. It's too late to discover if that would have caused alarm.

When she finds it, bright orange light bathes the interior. It's to keep the eyes relaxed, so that they don't forget what darkness looks and feels like. It stings Hanka's eyes most times. She squeezes them tightly shut before releasing them, giving her delicate slits time to adjust.

Unfortunately for both of them, the hut lacks any kind of provisions. There's only a couch and the lights. Hanka is grateful for that pantry exit. It meant they could stock up. She removes her backpack and her balalaika to pull out the small sachet. It's roasted grains and dried out fruits. With each bite, salty, sweet, and sour flavors burst into her mouth, the illusion of a complex meal just kissing her tongue. The greenhouses are a good thing—she will miss them.

"You should have told me you're a witch too," the technomancer says. "Perhaps I wouldn't have felt so uneasy."

"Uneasy?" Hanka raises a brow. "You're the one who barged into my room after I let you in."

"Yes, that's true, but—"

She waggles her finger. "No. I don't owe you anything. You're the one who brought the Kler to Tawerna." She keeps her tone steady. It's not an accusation, but a fact.

The technomancer softly grunts. "I don't know when they arrived. Perhaps before me. Perhaps after. It doesn't matter as long as they don't follow us. And they won't, right?"

Hanka swallows. "That depends on why you came to Tawerna. What's so special about it?"

"I could ask you the same thing."

"You don't get to." Hanka sighs as she sits on the couch, swirling her wrists to pop the tense bubbles caught in her tendons. Too long has passed since she used any magic. Her body protests. "I came to Tawerna because it was the farthest city I knew from where I had lived. Clearly, it wasn't far away enough."

"Tawerna is quite far from the border between the Kolebka and the lands beyond. I'm surprised I got this far, actually." Basia kneels on the ratty rug in front of Hanka, putting her heavy backpack down for a moment. "The Kler kept us out since the Zaćmienie. If they heard the slightest rumor of even one technomancer returning, they'd try to find me. If I were them, I'd be worried to have a technomancer so close to the Wieża."

"Well, I'm not a technomancer or a priest, so it's definitely not me they'll be chasing."

The technomancer tilts her head. "What are you?" When Hanka doesn't reply immediately, she repeats, "What are you, Hanka?"

Patryk should not have offered her name so freely—not that Hanka is the most uncommon of names, she knew two others at Katedra Wieszczów. But if anyone recognized her, it would be him. If he hadn't been with the Kler, she might not have tried to run away. She'd have tried to get him to stay with her. Instead, he came much later with his new brethren. The technomancer is no ally of the Kler, but that might mean she has a vendetta against the night-kissed beasts, and Hanka would rather be known as a bard for her own safety.

"I don't owe you that," she replies. "But since you know my name, perhaps you should offer me yours."

"That is only fair." The witch places a hand across her chest and bows. "My name is Basia, the last surviving member of a fellowship of technomancers seeking to slaughter the last of the constructs."

"There aren't any constructs in the Kolebka." Not living, anyway. Their unmoving husks lay crumpled and derelict within the bowels of the Katedra's libraries and conservatories. Hanka had seen one once and felt pity for the machinery now forced to keep the towns and the Droga running, the lights on and the rooms warm with vestigial magic. Stationary and obeisant, these were not the constructs the Kler feared from the world before. Tarnished gold struggled beneath the weight of the machinery and magic coursing through its engineered veins. They hadn't looked like they had ever moved. There were no legs or limbs, just cores that reminded Hanka more of carcasses discarded after a meal. The Kler showed them about the same amount of care.

"Oh, but there are," Basia says. "Three of them, from what I gathered. Hidden away."

"And you think they're in the Gwiedzna Wieża?"

"It'd be stupid of the Kler to put them *all* there, but I think at least one is. We call them Nadziemskie Strażnicy, the celestial guardians. There should be one for the stars, one for the moons, and one for the sun. We don't know if destroying them is going to do anything, but the Kler did promise my ancestors that once we'd hunted off all the rogue constructs, the lights would return."

"How would that happen?" Hanka asks. The Zaćmienie was considered an apocalypse, a controlled doomsday, yes, but an end to life as all knew it. But if biological miracles like her and Patryk are possible, perhaps undoing the night can be as well.

It's Basia's turn to shrug. "I don't know. We don't know the magic or mechanics that sealed it all away. It's what my fellowship set out to do, so I need to undo the night. Especially since I'm the only one left."

"I'm sorry to hear that." Hanka feels kinship, almost. Loneliness attracted to abandonment. Solidarity in solitude.

"I'm not the last *technomancer*. There's so many of us witches living beyond the Kolebka. But of those trained for this task? I'm the sole survivor." She avoids Hanka's gaze.

"I'm still sorry to hear that." Hanka has never had any companions to lose. Patryk had let her leave—and she had never expected to see him again.

"I suppose sympathy counts for something." Basia claps her hands on her thighs as she stands again. "So, what are we doing? Are we going to the Wieża? You said you knew where it was."

Hanka nods. She knows they need to go. She needs to learn why it was so dangerous for her to learn the scant technomancy she knows. The Kler would never tell her the truth of their world, even though she is a direct product of it. The answer has eluded her for so long, and it might just take her leading an outsider to that truth long withheld to find it.

CHAPTER FOUR

THE TOWER OF THE STARS

ANDRZEJ: WHO WAS AN INCREDIBLE SCOUT

WHEN THEY LEAVE THE hut, Basia breathes softly onto świecik, the glass charm that reminds her of the bulbs embedded in the Oświetlona Droga. It casts a faint light, enough to help her tread carefully, but not so much that it makes her an easy target in the Kolebka's darkness. When she was first alone, she relied for a long time on her hearing, to make sure that no beasts caught her unawares. She listened for both night-kissed and sun-embraced. The hissing and the clicking now resonate even when she dreams. Though she remembers the jingling of bells and the scratching of metal against long-unoiled joints and gears, Basia hasn't seen a construct since entering the Kolebka.

Before the Zaćmienie, the technomancers decommissioned their living machinery, allowing for a new age of the night-kissed. As punishment for not being able to control the sun-embraced constructs when they turned from machines to autonomous beings, the technomancers were cast out, tasked with traversing the world and destroying their work. And they thought they completed the task. The tamed constructs had been put to rest, the untamed destroyed. Perhaps it had been a mistake to not fully dismantle them all, but the Kler hadn't defined the terms of elimi-nation. The ones which wreaked enough havoc to raise the night-kissed Kler are no longer a problem. The technomancers met their part of the agreement. And they waited. They waited so long for the light to return.

It didn't. The Kler won't put an end to the darkness, but Basia will. She's come too far, learned too much, and knows this Wieczna Noc is not a natural thing. It's crafted from magic and a seizure of power. It promised peace, but no one accounted for the ways idleness and malingering make people fester. Ceaseless isolation will make humanity decline—she has already seen it in the lands beyond. But what has Hanka seen in the Kolebka itself that has her offering to be Basia's companion?

They don't speak to each other as they walk. With the Kler left behind in Tawerna, they're likely searching for any sign of two sun-em-braced witches. It's what she would do, and to keep themselves safe, they need to keep themselves hidden.

Hanka leads them to the bottom of a ravine where Basia cannot see the tops of the cliffs but the way her light bends and bounces off the sides suggests a change in scenery.

"We're almost there," the bard says, not pausing to get her bearings.

"How do you know?"

"You probably can't see it, but I can see night's kiss on the building from here. The priests need some way to find it themselves without having lights on all the time, you know. I've just never seen the miasma so...thick."

Is that how Basia would have done it? Cloaked an entire tower in magic only she and others like her can see? How is it that *Hanka* sees it? All that greets Basia's eyes is more of that obsidian void. The only way she knows of her surroundings is from the gentle glow of świecik, which is a spell meant to enhance, not conjure, fire. "That makes sense to me. Have you been before?"

"No, but I've seen it on a map."

"You've seen it on a map," Basia says, mocking.

A thunk echoes, followed by an, "Ow!" Hanka stops abruptly. "Found the stairs."

"I thought you just said that the building was covered in night's kiss."

"It is. Right there!" She points her right finger at the night above while bending forward to twist her left foot.

Basia cannot see a single thing, only engulfing darkness. "I suppose I'll trust you." If she can use the spells of the sun-embraced, why is it that Hanka can see that magic of the night-kissed? That may be the reason why the Kler seeks her as well. She too has a means of undoing their work.

Basia bends down beside Hanka and reaches forward where the bard stubbed her toe. Unlike the gritty path of the forest or the smooth cobble that makes up the Road, rough stone greets her fingers. She leans forward, casting her light. *Stairs.* Hanka has been so sure-footed this entire time so far; it bothers Basia that the bard missed something as obvious as this. Each step is a gradual climb, not the short jaunts found indoors.

"And the Wieża is at the top of these stairs?" Basia asks. There's no way for her to see the direction the steps go. Are they winding? Do they stop at storeys or simply keep going?

"It should be. I don't see any other way up there." Basia hears Hanka's joint crack and listens to the satisfied exhale upon pain's relief. Hanka straightens. "I'm ready. Are you?"

They climb. One cold foot over the over, they climb.

And climb.

And climb some more.

Basia has never done so much climbing—the entrance into the Kolebka is a flat tunnel through the mountains, sparing her fellowship a difficult trek up and down again. It wasn't intentionally built: nothing that was cast from the Kolebka was supposed to make its way back in.

This step-by-step isn't even the same type of climb as it would have been over the peaks and into the valley. No ropes, no repelling, no counter-balances aside from the way both of Basia and Hanka lean forward to make sure there's no risk of falling backwards. This is *infrastructure*, a relic of the time back when there was light, a world she has only heard of in songs and tales.

Just as Basia's thighs start burning, they reach the top. No more climbing, only walking. Gone are the refreshing scents of pine and crisp snow melt, replaced by the sharpness of metal and wet stone. She can't see past the circle of light afforded by świecik, an illumination that reveals large square stones, their edges blurred by layers and layers of stale snow.

"We're here," Hanka says, breaths heavy, bent over with her hands grasping her own knees. Basia wonders how much comfort she enjoyed or how much she had wandered before coming to Tawerna. If this exertion proves too much, what else can she not handle? Is this why Hanka demanded Basia protect her—for she lacks the stamina for the world beyond Tawerna's comforts? There must be something else. Or it might be that simple. The simplicity of stable life in the Kolebka has haunted Basia.

They take a few steps deeper into the courtyard, boots crunching against the drifts. Hanka grabs Basia's arm. "Did you hear that?"

"Hear what?" She pauses her own breath, following the path of Hanka's outstretched arm.

Just beyond the perimeter of her świecik's glow lays a mound of snow, hiding some kind of dome. Basia doubts it is a pile resulting of maintenance and shoveling. The rough shape of it suggests something living, and not another piece of architecture. It's a mass like a sleeping beast. As the two of them take more steps, Basia finally hears slow, rumbling murmurs carrying louder and louder across the gentle, frosty wind.

A tremor stops them in place.

Fluffed ice bursts with a great huff. The night-kissed beast rises, stomping on its six legs like blades. They connect at its ridged, carcinized body, a pedestal for the armored torso. It reminds Basia of the knights patrolling the realms beyond, silver armor reflecting świecik's glow in gleaming azure white.

Its paired arms hang low in its front. She cannot see if its hands carry shields or if shields are its hands. The metal-like plates are as tall as either Hanka or Basia. Sigils carved in onyx and black gold dance all along its body—memories of spells and activations. It mesmerizes as much as it terrifies. It seems too familiar to the sun-embraced's machines to be anything but a corruption.

"They wear armor now," Hanka says under her breath.

Basia ignores her own confusion. Her focus narrows on the beast before them. Against its size, the modest courtyard only feels smaller.

There's not enough space for the two of them to sneak by unscathed. She can't see if there's a door for them to run to.

She drops her backpack and frees her sword from its holster. She quickly whispers the magic to engulf the blade in its sun-embraced flame. The warmth licks at her face. Sweat beads against her skin.

The carcinoid night-kissed knight rears on its hind legs and brings them down, hard. It's enough to shake the snow on the ground, but not enough to falter Basia's sure steps. She promised to protect her new companion. She's been fighting ever since she arrived in the Kolebka, and though those previous beasts she felled did not wear any metal plates at all, they are all soft in the same places—the middle. The first of her fellowship to fall learned the hard way that seeking out anthropoid weaknesses spells death and ruin.

Basia leaps forward, tucking and rolling under the night-kissed beast. An awful, frustrated shriek pierces her ears as it despairs in being unable to find her. The eyes are too small and the head too incorrectly positioned to seek something beneath its belly. When she first came to the Kolebka, she would've thought the Kler sought better designs. Those expectations proved too lofty, and time and again their night-kissed have disappointed, much to her own personal advantage.

She swings the blade at the legs to her left. They lift and lower, fiercely stabbing at the ground, trying to find her. Basia evades and sears its outer shell with her burning sword. The beast teeters onto one side, exposing its soft, tessellated underbelly. With a smaller knife, she might have wedged the tip between the segments, prying the armor apart. Basia, instead, opts for destruction.

While the armored beast struggles to balance on its spindly legs, Basia angles her sword against the sharp curve of the beast's underbelly and lifts with all her strength. She thwacks at it like using a hammer in reverse. Meat and delicate white flesh sizzles beneath her superheated sword. She carves her way more like a chef than a butcher. The smell of roasted meat entices her stomach, teasing with its savory flavors not unlike a meal meant to be enjoyed while seated at a table.

As the beast falls on its side, guts and innards spill out. Hanka bends over, retching.

Basia's instinct for pity gets usurped by annoyance. She thought this companion might be the one person besides her to finally stand up against the night-kissed beasts that will be deterring their path.

At least this one thought to warn her of her need for protection beforehand.

THE BLADE MIGHT AS well have torn through Hanka's own stomach. But since her skin stays intact and whole, the only way for the disruption of her body to manifest is to come out her mouth. She'd gotten sick from food before, like the first time she ate too many competing textures at Tawerna after a lifetime of modest and meager meals afforded to the night-kissed at the Katedra. This silvery viscous material she's left atop the snow is nothing like her previous experience. She recognizes no food, only a thick liquid which should have stayed inside her.

Hanka clutches her chest. Her heart beats hard and fast. Pressing her fist against her sternum does nothing to calm it. The frenetic pounding hits her ears and temples. Her thighs tremble, unable to hold her up. She has never known pain like this. The pinches and spasms when other night-kissed beasts take damage or die has never felt so painful. It might be the proximity—Hanka had never been within watching distance of a beast falling or it could be because of her connection to the one who did the slaying. Hanka brought Basia to the base of the Wieża. Hanka, herself one of the Kler's creations, invited the danger.

She cracks her knuckles. She's frustrated that she couldn't get her hands around the neck of her balalaika, that her fingers could not brush against the strings. The beast should have been tamed and not destroyed. But she can't be cross at Basia about the violence. It's only natural for a guardian predator to attack intruder prey. Hanka had only borne witness to the most natural of encounters.

"Are you all right?" Basia asks from somewhere above. The way she chews out the words from her grit teeth suggests displeasure.

"You protected me."

"It's what I promised in exchange for you leading me here."

Hanka doesn't dare seek regret in Basia's tone. "I didn't realize the entrance would be a beast's lair." Why would that be on a map no one was supposed to look at anyway?

"It's a good trap. Keeps people away."

Hanka cannot confirm if the dusty piles in the courtyard's corners are ash, snow, or something else altogether. Her stomach churns thinking about what else lays in dormant hiding, though that might be the pain roiling inside her. She takes steady breaths. In and out. In and out. Like the first time she ever performed in Tawerna, back when things had been more normal, when the only pain was public embarrassment, not the guilt following a slaughter she didn't commit.

"Let's hope nothing else greets us on our way up," Hanka says. She doubts she can bear this pain again, especially if she's going to be useful to Basia.

"Up?" Basia cranes her neck.

Of course, the technomancer cannot see through the Kler's illusions like Hanka can, even with her little light. But Hanka sees the clear shape of the Wieża with its stained glass clock face. The glimmers of night's kiss do not touch its hands, only the numbers trapped in ice. What time it shows is truly up to her imagination.

The Wieża itself is shorter than she expected. The paintings and cartographic illustrations she had seen at the Katedra made it seem lean and elegant, a lithe structure to be seen across the world. This building might as well be the opposite: squat and looming, like the statues of winged creatures meant to keep birds off Tawerna's rooftops and gutters. Its sides are not svelte, but gravelly and pocked due to the uneven brick from which it was built. Where it lacks in height, it makes up for girth—a titanic structure dotted with pricks of light like eyes. It's too short to host other storeys—or, if it does, Hanka cannot see the openings for those windows. In Tawerna, like most Kolebka's single-building towns, the central structure necessarily served multiple purposes, apartment buildings, warehouses, and store fronts all bundled together. Only the Kler was allowed the privilege of having architecture be singular in its use. The Wieża is no different than the Kler's other real estate.

Hanka coughs, dislodging gunk from the back of her throat. It wetly hits the courtyard's stone. "It's not much taller than Tawerna."

"Are you serious?" Basia has already put herself back together. "Is it just the stairs that make it hard to get to?"

Her shoulders almost shrug, but she catches herself. Nothing she has learned of the Kaplice alluded to what they hide.

As the pain ebbs, whispered singing calls deep in the recesses of Hanka's awareness. The priests at the Katedra often spoke of the mountain's madness—where silence transforms into words of solace or offers the most base of temptations. That madness echoes in Hanka's head now, louder than any time she needed to be aware of her kindred's presence in the Kolebka's wilderness. Her heart and her mind have never been quiet, but it almost attempts to speak over Basia.

It does not want the technomancer to enter this sanctuary.

Forcing herself to speak past the inner cacophony, Hanka says, "Most people would not want to make the climb, no. Tawerna had stairs, but those stairs led to home and comfort."

"And these stairs lead to darkness and ruin."

"If that's how you want to think of it." Hanka doesn't want to let Basia believe that she too wants to partake in this violent rebellion. Simple disagreement with the Kler's Wieczna Noc does not necessarily mean she wants to personally be part of its destruction.

"I just want to know what the Kler hides. We killed every construct in the lands beyond, and yet..." Basia didn't need to finish the statement.

The darkness remains, smothering the world.

They walk past the night-kissed beast's fallen corpse. It smells like brine and moss, and Hanka doesn't want to think about it. The sickness returns, and she swallows it down instead of letting it come back up. She almost reaches out for Basia's hand, but the witch doesn't owe her that comfort—Hanka proved herself more than useless in their first encounter together against a night-kissed beast. Whatever awaits them in the Wieża will hurt Hanka again, and she will get sick. She won't let that momentary discomfort make her regret tasking Basia as her protector.

The door to the Wieża sits open, snow gently wafting from the ground outside onto the foyer inside. It can't have been open for long, as Hanka thinks either she or Basia would have heard it open. Either that, or, with the air so strange and the noise in her own head so loud, she didn't hear anything. There's no memory to scour.

Basia reaches into a pocket and throws out a stone. It hops along the inner masonry, disappearing into the dark, shapeless interior. Their closeness to the building must have dispelled the illusion. They wait a few breaths, hoping nothing reaches out to snatch the intruder. Hanka cannot sense another of her brethren, but she cannot tell Basia that.

"I should've done that in the courtyard," Basia says.

"Now you know for next time."

The witch quirks her lips. "Let's go inside."

As they enter, the glow coming off of Basia's charm shows an empty space, but not in a way that suggests abandonment, but a way that suggests no one had ever lived there at all. The floor seems too clean, the walls too bare—the Kler likes to mark its sacred places, and there is no evidence of them owning this one at all. They usually have their silver relics on display or make sure night's kiss leaves its mark on the upholstery and furniture. Hanka sees none of it, not even the furniture. The lack of magical energy reminds her of every corner of Tawerna, which had been left largely untouched by the night during her entire stay.

"Do you see anything?" Basia has not taken another step forward. She never put her sword away and now grips the hilt as if waiting for something to awaken and harm them.

"I don't." Hanka exhales. "What I mean to say, there's nothing for me to see in there. It's empty. It's like no one lives here."

"Why would anyone need to live here? It's completely out of sight of the rest of the world."

Hanka's own ignorance of the Kler's structures and strictures make it difficult for her to summon an answer. Instead, she admits, "They must have left something here." Something that made a burrow of this unattended space.

"How do we know that it's not looking for us?"

This Hanka also does not know how to answer. If there had been a beast here, it would have come to rescue its comrade. Those that share patrols and enclosures have sense connections like that—when one falls, the others find out. None had come to check on the knight in the courtyard. Hanka, being unique among the beasts as she is, would have sensed other movements. She does not. The only living thing she senses is the witch standing beside her.

Across the entryway, Hanka points to a doorway looking like a familiar shaft. "There's an elevator."

"That doesn't answer my question."

"If there was anything, I would tell you."

"Oh? Just like you had told me of the beast in the courtyard?"

Hanka pouts. "You didn't ask then." She doesn't want to suffer Basia's reaction if Hanka admitted to not sensing anything. "But, I'll try to tell you the next time I sense a beast."

"Did you sense the beast then?"

"No."

Basia doesn't react. Instead, she asks, "Does that mean you sense a beast now?"

Hanka shakes her head. "That doesn't mean we're alone now." All she can assume is that the Kler would not be foolish enough to leave somewhere so important completely unguarded.

Basia finally moves towards the doorway. "That's good enough for me. I'm operating on the assumption that there are, in fact, more constructs the technomancers haven't defeated. What I mean to say, Hanka, is that we're in agreement—we're not alone here."

It feels nice that they agree on something.

Basia reaches the lift first and pushes her foot out over the shaft. "The lift isn't here."

"Soon it will be," Hanka says as she pulls on a lever anchored into the wall. She's explored Tawerna's mechanisms enough to know that things built for the Wieczna Noc function similarly—simple physics tinged with magic borrowed from the technomancers.

Air swooshes from below as a plate scratches against the tight walls. The elevator screeches to a halt at their floor and the two of them step inside. Hanka puts her full weight on the pressure plate inside. The rumbling returns, and they rise. The vibrations remind her of sliding down the ladders—she practiced it so many times in case of a desperate escape. Her short hair tickles against the nape of her neck similarly. Her stomach curls up into her spine as her own trepidation catches up to her. Even though her pained exile should have inspired her to delve into what the Kler hides, she mostly wanted to live. To be herself instead of a creature ordained by an organization more interested in keeping its own power than bettering the world. While it's true that helping Basia learn her truth about the Kolebka's mythological constructs might set Hanka free as well, they could die here. All hope of anything more than mere survival doesn't even stand a chance.

The elevator grinds to a halt at the top. Basia steps off first, extending a hand to Hanka to help with the small lip of a step. It remains in its place even as the two of them put it behind them.

A large pair of doors greets them on this floor. They climb steps that lead from the floor to the too-tall ceiling. From Hanka's estimate, this must be the room with the clock face. Pressure tightens around her temples. No longer will she be ignorant of the world that exists under the Kler's curse.

Basia places her hands on either side of the seam connecting the door. With loud grunts, she pushes, digging her feet into the ground. Hanka narrows her eyes, checking if there isn't a mechanism or a spell she needs to undo to make this easier for Basia. She cannot find it. In fact, the door has the same absence of night's kiss as the rest of the interior. Basia's charm grants them all the light they see.

A gust blows in once the doors part. Basia yells, giving one final shove to create enough of a passage for the two of them. Unlike the two empty rooms they have come through thus far, the section of the interior closest to the door has the trappings of a bedroom raised on a platform. The sheets of the bed are neat, unused. A smaller door leads to a different space, likely a washroom.

Fabric dotted with glimmering stones hangs from hooks and rods all across the room, overlapping and cascading more like a waterfall than any material Hanka recognizes, giving the impression of more cloth than room. It's more material than Hanka has ever seen in her entire life, more than in all of Tawerna. She cranes her neck, trying to find where the fabric all connects on the opposite side, no doubt blocking the clock tower's face. After following several loops and turns, she finds cloth gathering along the ceiling on the far wall, looping up and down the hoops of an enormous baldachin. Her eyes settle upon a figure seated below these textile estuaries.

Though neither woman addressed it, the thing awakens. Hanka cannot see the night's kiss on it either. A scent like burning oak fills the air as the thing shifts beneath its blankets. As it shifts, a bald head emerges from the gaps and breaks in the fabric. It has no face, only smooth planes and a gate where she would place a mouth, nose, and eyes. A segmented column of chains pushes the head outward up along a sinewy neck, and its head turns until, if it had eyes, its gaze would land on Hanka and Basia.

"A long time has passed since I last had visitors." Its voice crunches, not ringing clearly like a person's should. It sounds manufactured, a collection of what words should sound like together, not at all smooth and spoken in living voice's uneven cadence.

The fabric shifts more, rearranging, refolding, twisting, and flipping. As the figure moves, fabric falls from the ceiling, dragging its weight behind it as it gathers around the body otherwise unseen. Most of it goes to wrap around the thing to give it a flesh-like bulk. Some threads and tassels stay aloft in the hoops, connecting to three pairs of wrists and one set of ankles like chains. She cannot tell if they are to restrain or if they are to puppet the thing.

All at once the stones caught in the fabric alight with the same suddenness as thousands of eyes opening. Night-kissed rings surround each one—it scares Hanka that she hadn't seen or sensed them before.

In a loud whisper, Basia says, "I cannot believe I'm setting my eyes upon the Strażnik Astralny." She drops her pack and grabs her sword's hilt with both her hands.

The name is perfect for the means of restraining the stars. "Astralny, right?" Hanka speaks clearly, hoping the bejeweled figure can hear her.

"What?" Basia snaps, arms trembling as she readies her attack.

"Strażnik Astralny—that is what you are?" This is not a night-kissed beast, so Hanka has no idea where her sudden desire for diplomacy stems from., except that it reminds her of the broken automaton she had discovered in Katedra Wieszczów, its final form realized, articulated, and mechanized.

"They didn't give me a name. They told me to hold the stars. And I think you are here to take them." The Strażnik Astralny's head twists sideways, getting a better look at Basia. "That sharp object. Such a pretty, sharp object. I would like to add it to my collection."

From beneath its many, many fabric folds, another half-dozen arms appear wielding giant blades like the abandoned halves of scissors. Each blade absorbs the light from the jewelry twinkling around them. Night's kiss transforms what should be glinting metal into rough, desolate steel. It lacks the beauty of Basia's blade—a beauty the Strażnik Astralny cannot have.

More cloth winds around all visible eight limbs. Long, elegant backward-bending legs support the structure of the Strażnik. It leaps forward straight towards Basia, the ribbons pulling on it like a harness. The fringes swish and fly around, casting strange shadows along the floor. Hanka realizes that it recognizes Basia as an enemy, but not her. Is it because of her lack of weapon? Or does it see that she is made of night's kiss and thus one of the Kler's creations?

If it had been the technomancers' creation, Hanka would be its target. This is clearly something also birthed by the Kler.

The only fighting Hanka had ever had to do involved summoning her own brethren to give her a chance to escape. It happened in the Katedra; it happened in Tawerna. In the Wieża, however, she stands too far up above the world with not enough windows to allow them to infiltrate. If she played her balalaika, no one would be around to hear it, like a tree falling soundlessly in the woods. No assistance would come. She doesn't deserve that assistance—the night-kissed beasts are not hers, nor anyone else's, to sacrifice.

Basia dashes forward, sword alight, burning with magic sparked from her charms. She weaves in and out of the fabric folds. The Strażnik spins, slashing sideways. There are no sounds of meat squelching nor metal grinding against metal. Instead, Hanka hears fire's familiar crackle and the scent of ash and burning fills her nose. View blocked by fabric, it's the only evidence she has that Basia is winning against the Strażnik.

But Hanka cannot let Basia fight this battle alone. It's Hanka's fault they were caught unawares—it would selfish and inconsiderate for Basia to do all the fighting.

She too drops her wares, kicking back her sack and letting the balalaika scratch the floor as she shoves it out of harm's way. It will not be her catalyst. She will draw her magic from her own flesh, much like her brethren. They consume each other, consume themselves, while the Kler simply siphons it from their blood.

Hanka yanks off her glove and places her left hand's first digit between her teeth, feeling around for the crevasse where the bones meet. There isn't enough of a well to draw from, and she's the only night-kissed beast around. The last time, when she escaped the Katedra, she had a night-kissed beast offer its flesh to her to heal her wounds. Without that assistance, she doesn't know if the skin, bone, and muscle will return on their own. She isn't sure how, or if, Basia can help her heal.

There will be no healing for anyone if they don't eliminate the Strażnik Astralny.

With a crunch, she cleaves her index finger, the flesh drying upon contact with her saliva and the cool air. The digit is thick as it hits her tongue, flesh dissolving and sliding thickly down as she swallows. The iron taste of blood briefly fills her mouth before quickly disappearing. The wound on that stump itches as it stitches together. Black liquid sluices down her hand, erupting in onyx flames.

Hanka curls her hands around the mass. She thinks of a blade attached to a rod, a straight shape ending in an arrow. Her right hand tugs at the air around her left hand's fingers, pulling more and more of this substance from the stump. The brightness becomes crisper, as if the pupil widens. She hears the rushing whispers of the darkness keeping the jewels in place upon the fabric. It's time to free them. She cannot tell if they fear or admire her.

She crafts a dark, crystal spear, frozen like ice. She grips its wet, shining surface as tightly as her gloved, aching hand will allow. She squares her shoulders and takes a firm step forward. Her elbow pulls back and snaps forward. The bolt careens into the Strażnik Astralny.

It hits its mark.

The fabric keeping it aloft recedes as it staggers. The Strażnik falls onto one knee like in genuflection. Its restraints pull tightly, lifting the body off the ground, yanking it far off the ground where the danger lies.

As it is absolutely not night-kissed, Hanka cannot hear or feel its pain. She summons another bolt and throws it. Patryk had taught her this art; she wonders briefly if he would be disappointed to see her turning it against the Kler.

Hit after hit, Hanka carves at the Strażnik. It takes them quietly, the only evidence of its pain torn cloth and fat, wet globules of oil dripping from its wounds. The liquid fizzes all over the floor, neither water nor sweat nor blood nor arousal. The flesh doesn't weep with magic the same way Hanka's does. In fact, the new injuries make its movements sloppy. The Strażnik teeters under the weight of its own blades and clothing. The fabric rolls and twists, tugging hard at the loops secured to the ceiling.

With every yank, the gems hit the floor as evenly as rain during a storm. They glint through the darkness. Their noise sparkles like chimes as they fall against the stones.

One more bolt has it severed from its restraints. This allows Basia to dash in, slashing and hacking at the clothing, cutting her way to the Strażnik's core. So much cloth billows that Hanka has a hard time following their movements. She's stopped casting bolts—she doesn't want to hit Basia. It takes a few baited breaths, but it does fall eventually. Its limp form sinks against the ground like discarded rags. Hanka wonders if this attire had been part of the construction. It must have been.

The Strażnik's tatters ignite in white light when they touch the scattered jewels, shining so bright they give off heat. She understands the Kler's need for their charcoal eye bands, for this light is far stronger than the power Basia had managed to summon with her charms. These glinting pebbles' power is immense—the Strażnik had been wearing the stars this entire time. Ever since the Zaćmienie. The Kler locked it up in this tower, never to be seen or heard from again.

Guilt and pity pluck at Hanka's heart. This imposed loneliness only ended in violence.

The Strażnik Astralny slumps. Basia climbs onto one of its many elbows and leaps into the air. With a final hack, her flaming blade slices through its chain-like neck. The head comes off clean. No blood, no water, no fluid bursts or sluices from the wound.

The cloth holding the Strażnik stiffens, then falls. It shatters against the ground rather than gently rippling. Hanka covers her eyes as white flames swallow the rags all at once. The collective eruption of light and magic break the clock face's stained glass, raining more shards against the world below.

Once the redness behind her lids subsides, Hanka removes her hands and looks up past the broken clock face. Millions of pinpricks float like snowfall up into the air. Mouth agape, she watches. They rise up and up and up. The sky is too far up to see what becomes of its darkness, but where the mass hits, glittering splendor remains.

These are the stars.

The Kler had lied—there are more constructs. Basia had told the truth—the Wieża did hide one of the lights lost to the darkness.

And if Hanka and Basia want to return light to the world, they only need to find and destroy two other Nadziemskie Strażnicy.

But first, they must bear witness to the wondrous and horrifying illumination now gracing the heavens above. The stars wink at the witch and the bard. Hanka believes it is in thanks. That is what she *wants* to believe. She won't let anyone take this beauty from her, even though it betrays everything that brought her into this dark world in the first place.

PART TWO: THE MOONS

CHAPTER FIVE

THE NIGHT SKY

MARISIA: WHO ALWAYS KNEW THE RIGHT DIRECTION

THE STARS WINK AND blink at them from the sky above. A silent tear rolls down each of Basia's cheeks. Fear still grips her body, but relief snakes its way through those coils. The remaining constructs weren't a myth. The rage hasn't made itself known yet; the Kler lied, but at least the loss of her fellowship wasn't for naught. She remains to free the lights. Hope sparks deep in Basia's chest—she was never the strongest or the most skilled, but she knows loyalty. She knows the mission.

Two more Strażnicy to defeat and the light returns to the world.

Basia hears a thud and a groan beside her. *Hanka.* She breaks her gaze from the heavens and looks at her companion. Basia no longer fears the sky and what the scattered darkness brings—she fears this small woman beside her, hunched over a self-inflicted wound.

Her lips tremble. She wants to ask, *What are you?* She wants to know why the Kler is after her. Why, if Hanka isn't a priest, she can cast such magic.

But first, comes pity. Basia kneels beside her and sees black blood pumping from the crude stump.

"I'm...sorry," Hanka manages. "It's been a while."

Basia hesitates to touch her. "Is this how the Kler casts?"

"No, they..." Hanka shudders, her cheeks puffing out. She doesn't retch. "They eat the beasts. They always have magic."

Basia swallows, uncomfortable. "So, that's what you did? Ate a bit of a beast?"

"To regain night's kiss, yes." Hanka curls over, yelling, "It fucking hurts!"

Basia cannot nurture her, cannot care for her like a nurse or physician. This goes beyond her ability to do anything, much less heal. "So, what's the remedy? How can I help...?"

Hanka turns her head, her blue eyes shining like crystals glazed with her own tears. "The thing in the courtyard. Bring me some of that."

With just the two of them and the Strażnik's tatters and their limp corpse, the clock face's room feels more the maw of a cavern than a feat of pre-Zaćmienie engineering, of which the only thing remaining is the bed within the small living space for whoever's job had once been to maintain the time.

"Do you have enough strength to get yourself there?" Basia says, waving her hand towards the bed in the corner.

Hanka nods. "Give me a moment, but I should."

"If there is flesh on the beast that we defeated earlier, would that work?"

"A beast in armor is still a beast." Hanka shudders as she tries to move her hand. "Sorry, I swear, I can recover from this."

"That I don't doubt." Basia doesn't know how truthful she is. Technomancers who lose their limbs and digits remain that way until their time comes. Regular humans, too. She thinks she even might have even seen a priest with a missing eye once, but the memory is hazy. It doesn't matter.

Hanka leans back, releasing her hands. Basia rises with her, ready to catch her should she stumble. No need. Hanka's breaths are heavy, but her feet are certain. "I think I'll be all right."

Basia gives her a nod. She takes her sword, but also checks for her smaller blades. They sit secure in their sheathes and pockets. All she needs is something to carry the meat back with her. There are a few sacks she collected from her fallen fellows—she has so many remembrances of her fallen fellows.

Each one of them left for the Kolebka with a resurrection stone. These crystals imbued with pure sunlight were the means of producing the constructs. But they had healing properties as well, and, in a strong enough dose, the power to reverse death itself. Basia hasn't used her own yet. It sits warm within a compartment in her breastplate. At some point, she'll have to tell Hanka about it. Not soon, not with this much uncertainty about what the bard is.

Basia twists świecik to create light for herself. The stars shine, but do not offer the same glow as the lanterns or the Droga. They won't help her in seeing the things she seeks. She pops open her pack and searches. Upon finding the fabric she needs, Basia goes back to the lift, descends to the ground floor, and leaves. The air outside remains as stale and frigid as ever, but she feels less alone with the centuries of stars casting their glow upon her. If there are more Strażnicy—more constructs, at all—are these scant lights enough to reactivate them? She doesn't think so. But if she were a member of the Kler, she would also take whatever precaution necessary. If there was even the barest chance that these soft glints would reactivate ancient monsters, she would hide them away too.

But they wouldn't have an effect on the shredded armor lying in the courtyard. It's not often that Basia returns to her kills. There had only ever been forward momentum, moving to the next thing, never looking back.

She admits to herself that the beast is beautiful. The armor has no blemishes, all smooth metal and clean planes. Whoever crafted it took pride in their work. In a sick way, Basia also takes pride in her work—despite the carnage, despite the unspooled viscera, there is an elegance to her butchery.

The cold keeps the rot at bay. The orange light help her see the edges of the carnage. Basia is almost proud of herself for the neatness with which she dispatched this creature. She reaches into its flesh. It squelches as her hands pull out essential organs not fit for consumption. Soft and squishy beneath her fingers, she doesn't let the texture make her sick. There are sea-faring peoples in the world whose primary diet consists of the ocean's fruits. This beast feels like a bastardization, a thing misplaced.

There isn't much raw meat; her sword had cooked most of it, leaving gray slime stained white and patched with black char. It could almost be appetizing. The smell makes Basia's mouth water. It's briny where it's raw and buttery where the heat hit flesh. She pulls out a folded knife and starts slicing, catching the delicate slivers in her palm. Not one for waste, she doesn't know how much to take. All of it so it can be dried for supplemental sustenance? Some of it and leave the rest to other beasts or things like Hanka? There were those back in the villages beyond the Kolebka who were experts in the curing and preservation of sustenance. Basia never spent time with them.

It's a pointless regret—best to eat it fresh and have the energy for the journey ahead. All that really matters is that they have the energy to meet the next Strażnik. They defeated one already. It's possible to defeat another.

As she carves the flesh, Basia wonders if this cannibalistic ritual of magical restoration is good for Hanka. The horror stories the techno-mancers told their children about their times of desperation always ended in madness as a result of consuming kindred flesh. Will this turn the bard into another animal? Will Basia need to seek another companion? These musings are unfair—she cannot assume to know Hanka's body and needs better than she does. It's arrogant and patronizing, and Basia has never had any parental instincts.

Trusting another might have been easier when the person at her side couldn't do magic. But it's the best she has for the battles ahead. Basia might as well make sure she also has her needs met.

WHILE BASIA IS OFF collecting meat, Hanka, lightheaded and dizzy, figures out a way to spark light in the unused fire pit. Charred wood sits there, dry and unused. It feels silly to strum a note of magic to activate it, but Hanka is too weak to siphon more from herself. As the spark leaps from her balalaika onto the hearth, the lift's familiar grinding graces her ears.

Wordlessly, Basia brings over a small, damp sack. They both look for a metal plate or something to get it onto the warmth. They discover the pokers and shovels for maneuvering the fuel. It's filthy, but not much dirtier than collecting the food in the first place. Basia doesn't tell Hanka to do anything as she carefully lays out the slices. They watch as the meat sizzles and bubbles. Hanka has never cooked before, but Basia seems to have some experience. They watch as the gray turns to white and pink. Hanka is fascinated by how Basia knows both when to flip it over and when it's done.

She passes a slice to Hanka. The flesh is sturdy and comes apart in her mouth with crisp, satisfying bites. The meat feels nice between her lips. She is loath to admit it, but it feels better than even the meals provided in Tawerna. There is something to be said about being in the presence of the food as it's made. Only certain people in Tawerna had such an honor. It's honest work. It's tender.

Hanka wonders if it's normal for the only sounds to be exchanged between them is her munching while Basia blankly focuses on her task. The meal cooks without magic, just heat and attention.

"So, I'll admit you were right," Hanka says after swallowing. "There are constructs in the Kolebka."

All Basia does is grunt in response.

"I'm sorry for doubting you. It was foolish of me. Why would anyone invent a fellowship that wasn't a pilgrimage?"

Basia still says nothing. If she doesn't want to talk, Hanka must simply accept the silence. So, Hanka decides it's time for her to share a bit of herself.

"You know, Patryk would do this for me. I was never one for cooking, only for eating. He was the one excited by all the meals. He really cared, actually. Always sharing with me, making sure that I had what I needed, sometimes at cost to himself." A small smile plays in the corner of her lips as she eats more.

Basia still says nothing but purses her lips and feeds Hanka another morsel. Perhaps it isn't the time to talk about herself, Hanka decides. If she talks about Patryk, she would need to talk about the Katedra, and considering that the Kler has already attacked Basia several times, it's not the time.

But even if Basia can't bring herself to say anything, be it selfishness or a razor-sharp focus on her own mission, her feeding of Hanka looks like care. Hanka will always take the appearance of tenderness over tenderness itself.

As the food fills her belly, Hanka's strength returns. Her head no longer feels like it's floating off her shoulders and the tremors throughout her arms and legs have stopped. Eating the flesh of a kindred makes a strange route toward feeling better. She eats until there is no more on the metal plate.

"Do you want me to prepare more?" Basia asks.

Hanka shakes her head. "Not right now. I don't want to make myself sick with fullness."

"It's a good thing I didn't butcher the whole thing, then."

"Perhaps we should? I've heard of methods to—"

"I don't think we have the luxury of that time. Or the ingredients." Basia glances at her. "How is your finger?"

Where there had been a stump, threads of darkness have begun to weave together in the imprint of a finger. It's not quite there yet, but it's coming back. It reminds Hanka of the violence within the Katedra. Beasts hurting each other, removing flesh and limbs, followed by feverish, lustful consumption, ending with their flesh stitched together with pale scars as the remaining echoes of wounds. It scared her then; it scares her now. It's why it didn't hurt when she chomped on her own meat. She couldn't see another way out, pain was going to come either way, and if this hurt prevented more permanent injury, so much the better.

The new digit's scaffolding moves as a finger should, though it glistens in the light. Hanka should remove her gloves completely and clean it, but it might have to wait until they reach a destination with plumbing.

She stands, steady, her legs doing the lifting that legs should do. "We should go see if there's anything we can learn here. I don't know why the Kler would keep an office with a Strażnik, but—"

"It's a good idea." Basia sets aside her cooking implement. "Where do you think it would be?"

Hanka scans the room. There's nothing to be seen that could even resemble an office. She goes to the other door and opens it. The space inside smells heavy with mold and a decayed musk she'd rather not think about. There will be no cleaning here.

"Let's take a look around the ground floor, there must be something there," Hanka says.

This time, Basia leaves her sword behind. Hanka doesn't think to bring her balalaika—after all, they're just wandering. If there's an office, there's an office. She's seen them before in the Katedra; the Kler keeps their most important wares and information inside tiny closets accessible only to them and their myriad keys. Hanka once tried her darkness magic as a lock pick; it didn't work, not like it did for the cabins throughout the Kolebka.

On the ground floor, they find several unopened doors. Basia kicks each one open. All abandoned. Not a piece of paper to be found or secret depository of books and tomes. A disappointment.

"There's nothing here," Basia says. A grunt more like a growl leaves her throat. "Why wouldn't they leave anything here?"

Hanka peeks into the rooms again. Much like the entrance, there is no hint that a person had ever lived here, none of the tells of domesticity. No stains, no scratches, nothing. It's as if the buildings housing the Strażnicy truly are mausoleums for beings that should never have lived in the first place.

"I don't think they intended for anyone to reside here," Hanka answers, shutting a door to remind herself that she's seen inside already. "Lock up the Strażnik, leave it alone."

Basia follows Hanka's lead in closing the doors. She leans against a wall, crossing her arms. "Where do we go from here?"

"What was your plan for entering the Kolebka?" The glare Basia gives her suggests she asks a bad question. "I mean, how was the fellowship going to get around and find that information?"

"Raiding towns, I suppose. Checking their archives—Tawerna had an archive, didn't it?" The question comes off as with the ferocity of an offense.

"If you wanted to kill the Tawerna Mistrz yourself, I suppose I should have let you, but I wasn't going to delay my own escape from the Kler with a murder. But, since you're still in the business of protecting me as long as I tell us where to go next, I think I have an idea."

Basia waves her hand for Hanka to go on. She hesitates for a second, because to her, it's obvious it's the same route she had dashed down during her escape from the Katedra, past the city of Stara Baśń. She didn't actually go inside the city walls, mostly because it scared her. In the Katedra, the Kler maintains a town of academics, of preachers, of people praying, despite the crimes against flesh and magic unfolding within the bowels of their research halls. In Stara Baśń, however, violence had been at the forefront. The Kler wears armor. The Kler has buildings dedicated to those who disagree with them, or so she heard. She never wanted to find out. Stara Baśń reminds the world of the Kler's might.

But Basia has a sword. Hanka can wield not one but two types of magic. Perhaps, together, they will be fine.

"There's a large town nearby called Stara Baśń. It's much larger than Tawerna, and I think we can find what we seek there."

"Have you been in Stara Baśń before?" Basia asks.

"I haven't. But I know it's big."

"And crawling with the Kler too, mostly likely."

"That's the one thing I know about it." Before Basia can issue a retort, Hanka says, "I know you still don't have a reason to trust me, and I cannot make any promises, but it's the best we've got. I haven't led you astray yet."

Basia grinds her teeth. Several different arguments and points play across her face in the way her brows furrow and soften. It charms Hanka; she'd never known anyone to be so expressive and unbridled.

A yawn catches Hanka first. Fighting, healing, and magic took a lot out of her. The warmth in her hips and shoulders suggest it's time for a rest. "Let's sleep on it."

Basia nods her head towards Hanka. "Sleep is not a bad idea, but I will keep watch. You're the one who needs to recover." Hanka looks at her hand. She's never had to do her own flesh stitching. Though progress is slow, it is still growth. It's something that sleep can expedite, her body becoming inert and only focusing on one thing.

"If you insist," Hanka agrees.

"I do, because we're not safe yet, but I can't have you be distracted by your own pain and discomfort while aggravating the Kler and their beasts."

"I agree. And that's why I'm sleeping on it." She winks, hoping that Basia takes something out of that playfulness.

She does, returning a grin. "All right, well, let's not dawdle."

They go back upstairs.

WHILE HANKA TUCKS HERSELF into the old sheets of the abandoned bed and swaddles herself like a babe, Basia sits at the bedside, eyes on the door of the lift. She dimmed świecik so it wouldn't disrupt Hanka's rest, but she did place another glowing stone to the left of the entrance. If someone entered, they would cast a shadow, if for some reason she didn't hear that now-familiar grinding of stone upon stone.

It shocks Basia how quickly the bard falls asleep. Perhaps it's the exhaustion, perhaps it's the injury, but almost immediately her breath slows as if she has found peace. This never happens to Basia. She rests in uneven fits whenever she can catch some shut-eye, and only ever enough to recover what scant strength she could.

The closest to rest she will get is the intermittent pattern in which her eyes choose to shut. It's a half-sleep that allows her to listen out for footfalls. Basia folds herself up and rests her chin on her knees. She should have removed her armor. It's tight across her chest and crusted with blood and other debris from her kills. Cleanliness had never been a virtue among the fellowship, a privilege reserved for longer rests in places free from danger, which might not be until after they leave Stara Baśń and eliminate the next Strażnik. But if that space is as abandoned as this one, then it won't be until whatever next residence they infiltrate.

This planning without a true plan is exhausting.

What also wears at Basia is the possibility of going to a Kler stronghold. She questions her vigil. Despite her own fears about an ambush, she should also rest. Her head should be nestled in that pillow beside Hanka's. Perhaps she could even cast a passive spell to accelerate the healing. It's what she would do for a human, but Hanka has proved she's anything but. She also doesn't seem loyal to the Kler; though they were after Basia, Hanka had attacked them with no regards for her own safety.

Basia should have let Hanka tell her about Patryk. She should have provided more correct responses to show that she was listening and wanted to hear more. If Basia had to guess, it was Patryk himself who had revealed Hanka's name. He's the key to unlocking the truth of what Hanka is. There will be other opportunities for that conversation. Though she doesn't know the bard, Basia should at least give her a chance to explain herself, unlike Basia who had simply taken the first possible opportunity. Subtlety and patience weren't necessarily her skills.

She had never put so much faith and trust in someone else's experience since the beginning of the fellowship. Once they had begun to fall, her remaining companions served simply as a means for her to be resurrected—which is a discussion she needs to have with Hanka as well. But if Hanka can fight with not one but two types of magic, perhaps there will not be a need. Despite these moments of weakness and strange displays of unusual biology, Hanka has been reliable. Her best companion yet, better even than Mirek.

The stars begin to disappear from the sky. Before panic sets in about the Kler having already created another Strażnik with which to bind them, Basia remembers that the days would cycle between light and dark, night and day. It had been a legend of the world before the Zaćmienie. She hopes she'll get to see it herself.

She doesn't expect to survive that long, not if every Strażnik has a will to fight and the one person she can rely on is the one also taking her to places teeming with those who want any technomancer dead.

CHAPTER SIX

OLD TALE

ADAM: THE PARTY-BOY WHO SHOULD'VE BEEN LEFT TO HIS VICES

THE ROAD TO STARA Baśń is as cold as it is lonely. The bard and the witch speak no words to each other, guided only by Hanka who can see in the dark, with Basia keeping her own lights dimmed to prevent attracting any unwanted attention. It did cross Hanka's mind that the stars could reawaken constructs, if they run on lights, but it seems that fear from the Kler had also been exaggerated.

What mesmerizes Hanka most about their journey is not just the great distance traveled, but also the way the stars appear and disappear when enough time passes. It's the first time Hanka had ever been aware of it. Things change and happen; there's a measure of length. The Zaćmienie had brought night and night remained. No longer, it seems. There are cycles again. Though she doesn't know if the starless sky is true night or if that's where day should be. Excitement roils in her stomach as she thinks of the possibility. It's the idea of colors that excites her most. She has no notion of what day could possibly look like, only the rumors she heard in the Katedra and the brightness with which Basia casts.

They find the Droga, its winding light snaking through the Kolebka. They don't dare step on it. Instead, Basia and Hanka traverse alongside it. Not once does Basia question if Hanka is taking them the right way. At intersections, signs point in the right direction. They find one indicating left for Tawerna and forward towards Stara Baśń. The numbers beside their names are meaningless—those distances are largely for the Kler's benefit and those who had been ordained to travel between the towns. Trade was limited and infrequent; Hanka does not worry about meeting merchants. In fact, if she hasn't seen one yet, it's likely she never will. In that there is a blessing.

Where the Droga leads to a town, there is typically a kind of guard's gate, shining, waiting to examine every person entering. From what Hanka knows of the Stara Baśń, it has two: one where the mouth of its lake meets the Droga, continuing onto a brilliant, sparkling bridge where it connects to a twin gate house embedded in the wall surrounding the town. The town itself sits upon the lake, inverted on a cone that twists into the sky, its tip a cloud-piercing point. At least, that is how the illustrations on all the maps made it seem: elegant and fortified.

Instead, when they reach Stara Baśń, darkness interrupts their path like a broken branch.

Even with her ability to make out shapes in the night, Hanka cannot see a thing of the city. Where grand ribbons of the Droga should swirl in overlapping roads and layered terraces throughout the city, there is darkness, the absence stark against the glittering skies. She expects the windows to at least have some glow coming from them, indicating that there are living people within. Instead, there is nothing. She cannot see the spires, the buildings, no hint that a single person had ever been here.

"You don't see anything either, do you?" Basia asks, softly.

There are glimmers of orange—firelight—obscured by towers and uneven rooftops. She narrows her gaze towards strange shapes hanging off the sharpened undersides of Stara Baśń's defensive towers. Bodies, she realizes, broken and beaten.

She catches the scream in her hands before it escapes her mouth. She doesn't know if they're human or Kler and it terrifies her to find out. A conflict had taken place here, and she can only think that her escape from the Katedra could have precipitated all manner of retribution.

Though Hanka herself had never set foot in Stara Baśń, the Kler could have conducted an investigation, accusing everyone of harboring one of their beasts. Where else could a night-kissed beast have gone? To another bastion of the Kler would have been silly, but the Kler may not have thought that.

Not all towns had the Kler, as evidenced by Tawerna. She specifically ran there because it was safe for her to do so. The Kler only ever visited on the occasional pilgrimage, and they never graced the populace, except for when they realized Basia had made her way there. Hanka remained in Tawerna because no one had ever asked any questions about her origins, never questioned her eyes, nothing. People in the towns learned long ago that privacy was the most effective form of protection. Towns who evaded the Kler's direct control were largely considered the safest. They stayed furthest away from the progenitors of the night itself.

"What is it? What do you see?" Basia asks.

"Nothing," is the word Hanka manages. Not because it isn't true, but because it's the easiest answer.

"Are you sure?" Basia isn't letting Hanka forget about not seeing the beast at the Wieża's base.

Hanka exhales. "There is a town here, it's just hard to see, and I don't know why I can't see it."

Basia places her fingers gently on Hanka's chin and lifts her head. "Is there something wrong with your eyes?"

There shouldn't be; there's no reason her vision would have changed at all since leaving Tawerna. "I think something happened here. Something really bad."

"The kind of bad that would ruin a town?"

"The very kind." Hanka inhales and lets out another shaking breath. "What do you want to do? There should be a way in via the drainpipes, but..."

"But what?"

"I'm afraid of what we're going to find."

"I'm willing to find out if you are. If not, where else are we go to?"

The last place Hanka wants to take Basia is the Katedra. The Kler will kill them both on sight there, Hanka for escaping in the first place, and Basia for the crime of violating the terms of exile. It's not a possibility she's willing to entertain. "I suppose we don't have any other choice. But what about your pack? I don't know how deep the lake is and—"

Basia silences her with a kiss on the nose. "I promise my pack will be fine. There must be some part of the lake we can traverse on foot, right?"

Hanka turns to face the placid, mirror-like waters of Baśńi Oko. The lake is shallow, from what Hanka remembers reading. Stara Baśń is not known for fishing or trading because of how the waters rise and fall with rainfall, but the entire basin has all been snowed over. Had the return of the stars warmed the world up enough to invite melt?

"Here." Basia gives Hanka a stone glimmering orange. "It's one way we checked depths and heights as we made our way into the Kolebka."

"What do I do with this?"

Basia takes Hanka's hand, positions herself behind her. "Have you ever skipped stones before?"

Hanka shakes her head. She has never been close enough to any body of water to be able to do anything fun with it.

"That's all right. You're going to angle your hand like so." Basia adjusts Hanka's wrist so she holds it at an angle, flattened to match the frosty shore upon which they stand. "And then flick and release."

With the gesture, they cast the stone together. It skims the surface felted with hoarfrost, bouncing once, twice, before floating down. Its glow dims quickly.

Basia clicks her tongue against her teeth. "Too deep. I don't want your balalaika to get wet."

"Is it too deep for us to cross at all? I can always hoist it over my head."

"Yeah? And then what happens when we have to climb a pipe or something to enter? What happens to it then?" When Hanka has no answer, Basia says, "Let's keep finding our way around."

Together, they throw about a dozen stones until Basia finally declares a spot. Hanka had entered Tawerna through the front entrance, not the side where the city disposed of refuse. Even through the dark, she can see the water pumping off the side of Stara Baśń, a spewing mass of liquid that only makes her stomach curdle. The smell reaches her nose even where they stand on the shore. That is human waste, and she wants to be nowhere near it. She narrows her eyes some more, looking until she sights a ladder that leads directly to the pipe. Nothing defends the opening, except for the bodies.

She swallows hard. The need to purge her stomach will only intensify the closer they get.

"I'm going in first," Basia says as she adjusts the straps to her pack so it sits high on her broad shoulders. "If anything attacks, I can take care of it."

Her willingness to protect Hanka makes her heart skip a beat.

The two of them slide down the chilled, muddy shore. Broken ice dusts the shore, the water not quite cold enough to be frozen, but frigid enough to instill a bone-deep ache. Basia doesn't shudder when she wades into those depths. When Hanka sees that the water only reaches to the tops of her thighs, she follows.

Cold sinks its claws into her skin. She holds back a yelp—no emergency, just the surprise. It reminds her of when a more animal-shaped night-kissed beast bit her. All the warmth in her body sluices out, her muscles seizing, but she must press on. Each step feels harder than the last as the lake's bottom squelches beneath her boots. She cannot tell if it's sand or something worse, detritus built up from waste and the dead, stagnating at the bottom of the lake like a bog.

She hates that each step brings her closer to that foul, foul smell.

She's jealous that Basia cannot see its origins. Bloated bodies wrapped in the Kler's garb bob along the surface. Their skin has gone pearly white. Bodies should not be discarded like this. Despite the sins the Kler has committed against light and the natural order of the world, even they have the decency to show honor to the fallen. If this is how Stara Baśń treats it dead, how poorly does it treat its living?

What's worse, though, is the growling, splashing, and munching coming from within the walls. Hanka doesn't recognize it as her kindred's song. This is no song at all. This is different, for there are still creatures in the world that are neither night-kissed nor constructed. The beasts crawling around and searching for food around the only entrance they know of into Stara Baśń are simple rats, waiting to gorge on the feasts discarded by civilization. From the corner of her eye, Hanka sees that they had grown large from devouring what remained of the citizenry themselves.

"You hear it too?" Basia murmurs, soft enough not to catch the creatures' attention.

Hanka doesn't nod, instead saying, "I do."

"Follow me, I don't want to get into a fight." Basia reaches behind to catch Hanka's hand. It's this small gesture of comfort that returns the bravery to her cold bones. Basia leads her, guiding her in winding patterns such that the squeaks stay far to either side. It's nice to not have to rely on her own senses.

There's comfort in knowing that someone else is so willing to take the initiative.

"We're close." Hanka sees the ladder. Overgrown plants hang off its sides, dripping like stalactites.

It takes a few steps, but Basia crawls up onto the platform upon which the city stands. She turns around and pulls Hanka up, that strength making her feel gentle like some kind of princess. The fetid stink seeps into her trousers, soaking into her shoes and socks, and she resents that there likely will not be a chance to get it cleaned until they defeat the final Strażnik, assuming they survive the encounter.

From high above, they hear a rush of water. Another body falls out of the pipe and into the abyssal pool below. Hanka and Basia do not stay and wait to see what carnage the rats wreak upon the poor sod. They have no choice but to hear it, however. Paws claw, rend skin, and tear into muscle. It reminds Hanka of the brood, of how her and Patryk's kindred might eat. It's a memory she thought she left far behind, but it surfaces much like the broken bones and limbs that the rats chew off.

Basia goes first, but they climb up the ladder together, careful not to slip and become centerpieces for the banquet below.

Stara Baśń smells worse than its sewers, and Basia isn't at all sure how that could possibly be. Not only is there a rancid musk that makes her face scrunch, but black smoke rolls and billows across the street as they climb up the ladder. It's a strange side street that they have entered, alongside a canal which seems more an aqueduct than a causeway for the town's waste. It's really a city—at least, if she were to assign the definitions of the world beyond the Kolebka. Thousands of people would have stacked on top of each other, if the number of windows indicate anything.

Now, the only lights within Stara Baśń are the flames burning through the corpses. No lanterns. No lamps. Only fire.

Basia never thought she would ever feel pity for the Kler, but seeing their bodies lying in haphazard heaps, smoldering like makeshift funeral pyres, coaxes sadness for them. Why had these bodies been burned while the others had been discarded below? Why do these people get to have cleansing fire chew through their flesh instead of becoming a meal for engorged rodents?

As much as she pities them, she feels safe in equal measure. These enemies of the Kler are not necessarily her friends, but whoever led this revolution might be an ally. They have the same goals, for whoever launched this uprising wants the Kler to pay for their sins. All she wants for herself and, by extension, the other technomancers, is for the Kler to fulfill their end of the bargain and return the celestials to the sky now that the constructs are gone. Her fellowship did not come to the Kolebka to commit eradication. The Kler started that first, and they will soon discover that it simply isn't possible to cast out all the technomancers.

"I don't like this," Hanka mutters.

Despite the resentment and hatred she feels for the Kler, Basia agrees. Whatever happened here isn't right. It's retribution. It's not righteous. It's a different kind of eradication. It's not one that can be met with equal force and similar outcomes. "Let's focus on why we're here. You know the Kler, where do they keep their archives?"

Hanka turns around, tilting her head up. "They're always at the top, looking down upon the world."

Basia squints and resents that she has the measliest of human eyes despite her own proficiency in light-based magic. There is nothing for her to see. If there are bodies burning up above as well, their glow does not reach this lowest tier of Stara Baśń.

"We just have to go up again, huh," is all Basia has to say.

Hanka nods with a grunt, agreeing. "I don't know the way, though. I'm not a priest."

"And thank fuck for that. Let's go find somewhere else to be."

They hold hands again. Basia enjoys the feeling of Hanka's hand in hers. The bard's hand is cool in a way that soothes the tension in her palm. But it's more for Hanka's benefit. If her guide feels safe, then Basia sees success in the next step of the mission. They just need to find more information.

She glances at each smoldering pile, and, judging by the melting silver and charred fabric, these fallen are all Kler or the people who served them. From what she knows of the people in the lands beyond the bounds of the Kolebka, they would not have taken up arms unless the Kler forced them to fight on their behalf. The same seems to be true here. The homes lining these streets sit darkened, either because their residents are asleep, feign sleep, or want nothing to do with the skirmish outside. The Wieczna Noc has ruined people's sense of responsibility but enhanced their self-preservation. If Basia hadn't found her own conviction in the fellowship's task, she too might have faked abandoning her home when they knocked on her door.

The flaming bodies guide them as they make their way towards what Basia hopes is the centrum of Stara Baśń. Most towns are constructed with a central plaza, no matter their size. Trade and markets have to take place somewhere.

But as they finish traversing the back alley and make their way into the plaza, they see the cause of the violence. Surrounded by three guards in makeshift armor stands a man drenched in blood. A hood not unlike the Kler's covers his head, a sword in one hand and a staff in the other, and as he turns around, it seems his clothing had been the site of a skirmish. Injuries or the strain of battle have torn his shirt in half. Fabric doesn't stand a chance against blades and magic.

Before Basia can shout for Hanka to run, more guards descend upon them. They pull the two women apart, shouting commands at each other. Basia reaches for Hanka, but it's no use; these defenders are simply too strong. Her soggy boots slip and slide against the cobbles. The fight within her dies quickly—they aren't dispatched immediately, which means there is a chance to talk to whoever is in charge here.

"What do we have here?" The man in the ruined clothes approaches them, taking steps on his tall legs like a lanky doll, uncertain on limbs too long for his frame. He moves carefully to keep his flat breasts covered, but they rebel and escape from beneath his ripped shirt. Round pink nipples harden in the night air, and Basia cannot tell if it's a display of vulnerability or a challenge.

The sword he sheathes is not one Basia recognizes, but the staff he leans on reminds Basia of the Kler's weapons. Its surface, however, is cracked and devoid of gems. She wonders if he's a priest or just used one of their weapons as a bludgeon.

"Stara Baśń wasn't expecting a pilgrimage." He bows his head forward. Even through the darkness swathing Stara Baśń, his green eyes glow wet and bright in the funereal pyre light. He looks down at them from his sloped nose. He's taller than both Basia and Hanka, towering over them without having to change anything about his posture.

Unfortunately, Basia's arms are held firmly behind her back. She wonders why the guards don't kick the back of her legs as well, make her kneel and complete her humiliation. They don't; they keep her firmly upright.

"We are no pilgrimage," Basia replies. She tries to keep the fight out of her voice, but the gravel in her throat and through her grit teeth has something else to say.

"Then why the blade?" His voice comes out almost singing. He is drunk on his own power, if he is the one who caused all this violence and destruction.

"The blade is for my own protection. And hers." Basia tries not to look at Hanka. If harm should befall either of them, Basia wants to take the brunt of it. She's the one who uprooted Hanka from her safety, from the little life she carved out for herself.

"One blade for two? How interesting." He bends forward, making his blood-splattered hood level with Basia's. "So, you're the guardian? Is she a priest you're protecting?"

"Neither of us are members of the Kler, if that's what you want to know."

"You're not clad in black and silver, of course I don't think you're priest of the Kler. Which only makes you that much more interesting to me."

The smoke tickles the back of Basia's mouth and she coughs, loudly. Her ribs grip her lungs, forcing air through her throat. There is dust in there which begs to be dislodged. It's nothing a bit a water can't fix, but even such slight relief is too big a request in her position.

"So, if you aren't Kler, what are you?" He tilts his head.

Basia glances at Hanka. Her blue eyes plead for her not to say anything. The truth is strange, the lie she's given does not explain her weaponry or the fact that they smell like Stara Baśń's refuse because they were never supposed to be in there in the first place. They're not residents. They're not travelers. They're something no faction within this darkened world could have seen coming.

Without any other options, Basia tells the truth. "The Kler's greatest enemy: a technomancer."

"A *technomancer*," he says. He then laughs. "The Mistrz before me mentioned technomancers, even accused me of being one myself. Absurd, that wanker kept such a tight grip on everyone who lived here. It was a city of his spies. Naturally, if he thought me a technomancer, he should have known the entire time I lived here, even before I was a man. But you two, I don't recognize at all. You're not from here."

"No, we're not. We traveled a long way to get here. Please, we truly mean no harm." It's far too soon to determine that truth, but Basia needs him to trust her—to trust *them*. "Well, no more harm that had already been done."

"*We*? Or do you mean, 'I'? Your companion, I'm sure, is more than capable for speaking for herself."

It's Basia's turn to pleadingly look at Hanka. Basia has this negotiation under control. Hanka understands and does not speak.

"So," says the Mistrz, "a bard traveling alongside a technomancer with a sword. I cannot say I've seen that before. In fact, it sounds like something out of a story. And I'm sure you two have quite a tale to tell." He glances to his guards.

"Are you sure, sir?" the one holding Basia asks.

"If they decide to fight, you can just restrain them again. Clearly, they weren't prepared the first time."

The grip on Basia's wrists releases. She rubs one wrist, glaring at this supposed Mistrz. She doesn't want to kill him, nothing about him suggests a threat—at least to them. He's just trying to protect the people of this town from the Kler, even though their own fear of the darkness outside ensures their security in calmer times. The harder Basia believes that they are allies, the better this outcome will go for all of them.

Until Hanka opens her mouth and says, "We're not on the side of Kler. The opposite, actually. We're on a different kind of pilgrimage—to bring the light back to the Kolebka."

Fear nips at the base of Basia's neck. In so few words, Hanka shared so much with a stranger. Basia keeps the frustration at bay; she too had been dangerously honest with the bard upon meeting her in Tawerna.

"To bring the light back?" The Mistrz's pink lips split into a wide smile that deepens into belly laughter. "That is the most delusional thing I have heard since learning that the Kler's own hubris put the lights away in the first place. You two? A pair? To bring the light back should take an army."

Hanka straightens. "Well, we're an army of two. We eliminated one Strażnik already."

"A Strażnik?" He looks up at the skies. The stars are still veiled, their time has not come around again. But the way he stares at the sky suggests that he knows just how the heavens have changed. No longer is this the Cradle of Eternal Night. The stars are back. "If I were a learned man, I'd guess that to be the name of the means by which the Kler dims the lights. Is that true?"

Basia admits, "It is. We triumphed against the Strażnik Astralny not long ago."

"It wouldn't happen to be when the stars first appeared in the sky?"

"Precisely then." Basia wants to run. This conversation is going nowhere, but they have two more Strażnicy to eliminate, and they stink, and they need to rest as long as Hanka still doesn't have a finger.

"It's interesting." The Mistrz crosses his arms. His torn sleeves reveal hairy limbs as coated in blood as his clothes. "It's only been recently that I learned most people didn't think the darkness to be natural. But to see others from outside Stara Baśń feel the same way? I feel like I came out of a dream."

The aches permeating Basia's travel-weary joints and hips remind her that this is very much reality. "Funny you should call it that. A dream. My people have a similar vision of a world without the Kler's scourge. It seems we are aligned in our goals."

Hanka hides her injured hand. "I think so as well. We're looking for more Strażnicy. We thought the fortress of Stara Baśń would have the answers we seek."

The Mistrz says, "Here, there are answers to questions I didn't even think to ask, little bard. With the Kler gone from Stara Baśń, there is no more fear about what one can and can't learn about the truth of this world."

"You're not going to execute us." The way Hanka asks suggests a statement, not a question.

"I may change my mind about that depending on what you have to share with me, but first, why don't I arrange for some baths and a dinner for you? I think we have much to discuss and much to learn from each other."

THE BAŚŃI MISTRZ'S ESTATE sits at the base of Stara Baśń's central tower. It is a three-tiered structure, each floor smaller than the last. The guards confiscate their packs and weaponry, shoving Basia and Hanka into a communal washroom in naught but the filthy clothes sticking to their backs. It's a cavernous wooden room with several stone basins with water bubbling from the minerals used to clean it. Round lamps hang from the ceiling, casting the room in a gentle honeyed glow. Rotund boilers hiss in the corners, bathing the space in warmth. Tawerna was both large and tight-knit enough to afford everyone their own place for cleansing. Hanka isn't sure if she'd enjoy having to bathe with others around.

But with Basia there it isn't so bad. They undress wordlessly, depositing both their trousers in one of the pools, staining the water brown with muck that Hanka doesn't want to consider. Though they have their backs turned to each other, Hanka cannot help casting furtive glances at Basia. It's the deep lines shaping her legs. It's the grooves in her back, calling attention to her shoulder muscles. It's the downy fur within her pits, wishing to be licked.

It's the scars and faint bruises that she wants to kiss.

Hanka wonders if the Mistrz is dressing them up for slaughter or if he truly intends to deliver on his promise of exchanging information. She hasn't been near a Mistrz before, generally keeping her distance from the man running Tawerna for fear that he would report her to the Kler. Here, it's the Kler that was met with violence. Perhaps they are safe by virtue of not being priests, but at the same time they might not be safe because they're not residents of Stara Baśń, mere intruders.

"Do you need help with anything?" Basia asks, breaking the silence.

Hanka opens and closes her mouth, eventually landing on shaking her head. She knows how to clean herself.

"How's that finger?"

Hanka looks down at her hand. In the time since leaving the Wieża, more threads of smoke have woven together into meat that obeys the commands sent from her bones. Patches of pale skin have also appeared. She folds it and extends it. "I can't quite feel it yet, but I know there's something there."

"Good. Would you mind helping me scrub my back? I can't quite reach."

A furious blush takes over Hanka's face. She attributes it to the steam and the heat. "I can do that."

Basia picks a pool to sit herself in. If Hanka weren't so frightened and so skeptical of this entire mission to undo the bleak darkness that smothers the world, she'd admit that Basia is beautiful. Perhaps rough around the edges, but what blade isn't? Even the sharpest swords have indents.

Hanka takes a glass carafe of oil from beside the pool and pours some onto her hands. It's silky and soft, smelling sweet and fresh unlike anything she had experienced as a mere bard, far sweeter than any flora she encountered in her escape from the Katedra. There were flowers in Tawerna's greenhouses, but they had been accessible only to the Mistrz. She had sneaked in once and immediately understood what the secrecy was about. The petals fell off at the slightest touch. Dust-like pollen burst forth with slightly too strong a breath. It had intoxicated her. It was in that pleasure she learned that only those in charge of the Kolebka's rule could luxuriate in that softness.

How Stara Baśń's bath house has access to such delicacy is beyond her.

But the oil looks perfect on Basia, making her paleness glow as warm as her skin feels beneath Hanka's fingers. The muscles spanning her back only give when Hanka presses her fingers as firmly as she would on the neck of her balalaika. She realizes just how sturdy Basia is. Whether the witch wanted to develop such toughness remains to be seen. It's not the point. The point is to clear the grime off her, a slight reprieve offered as they wait for further summons from the Baśni Mistrz.

As Hanka rubs small circles, Basia arches her back, releasing an airy groan. "Keep going." It comes out like a purr. She has never heard anything so contented.

Blushing, Hanka doesn't stop. She moves her massage down Basia's shoulder blades, easing the pressure when her fingers glance Basia's ribs and she giggles. The flesh there feels as stiff as the bone, and Hanka applies more oil to her fingers. Grime mixes with the slick. She dips her hands into the pool and splashes water against Basia's back. Basia cracks her neck, the joints snapping, releasing tension. "Thank you so much."

Hanka dips her hands into the water, rinsing them. Dirty bubbles rise to the surface, floating along until the drain drags them to the pipes below.

"Here, let me do something for you." Basia pats the space next to her, inviting Hanka to sit.

The witch takes Hanka's foot in her lap, grasping the side with one hand as she takes the same carafe and dribbles the oil along Hanka's skin. Her eyes maintain a serenity of focus that Hanka has only seen in musicians.

Blood rushes between her legs. Wetness drips from her slit as Basia's callused fingers press around her sole and slip between her toes. It tickles, but she doesn't dare let her foot flinch back. Hanka is the one who promised "later," and it's Basia that is following up. The witch's hands coax suds along Hanka's calves, loosening those tangled pale leg hairs. She can't help but notice the way Basia's own dark body hair wafts in the water gently churning around her ankles.

Basia keeps her eyes on her work, only glancing up at Hanka whenever she whimpers. She wants to be touched so badly. Hanka wants to spread her legs and show Basia the way her cunt drools. Perhaps its smell will entice her.

The pink splotches kissing the top of Basia's cheeks suggest curiosity or embarrassment. She gently takes the foot and deposits it into the bath. "Give me your other leg."

Hanka obliges, offering Basia her other leg. The one cleansed feels loose, strong fingers having kneaded the knots and coiled up tension, smoothing Hanka's muscles. Instead of just focusing on her foot, Basia's hands crawl up her calf. Hanka winces. Basia's fingers roll over the pulsing pain.

"Does this hurt?" Basia asks, her fingers prodding at the spot.

Whatever tangle happened there slowly undoes Hanka's arousal. "It does, I don't know what happened."

Basia scoots back, straightening Hanka's leg. "Tell me when it hurts, and I'll stop. Cramps like this aren't uncommon." The witch palpates the calf, starting at Hanka's sensitive ankle and moving up along her leg. Hanka yells when her fingers press into the knot again.

"I fear we might've walked too much," Basia says, with a tenderness as if she expects the words themselves to reach the fibers beneath Hanka's skin. They don't. More pressure doesn't do anything for it either.

It surprises her that her night-kissed body can experience such pain. None of her kin have been known to carry such discomfort. She doesn't remember Patryk ever complaining about such things. It's likely because the farthest they ever walked had been in repetitive circles around the Katedra's grounds, feeling the grass and stone beneath their feet. Free from the confines of their imitation of humanity, free from the coldness of the nursery's cage. Free, like people should be.

Free to roam, like people once did when the lights still graced the world.

Basia's hands have begun to inch further up towards Hanka's thigh when a knock at the door jolts both of them out of their skin and back into the room. Into the steam, reminding them that they are guests or prisoners in Stara Baśń. The serenity lasted too long for anyone's liking.

Basia stands, wraps herself in a towel, and approaches the door. Someone who must be a servant stands there with several folded items of clothing.

"The Mistrz thinks you might want to be comfortable at dinner," is all the servant says as they hand off the garments to Basia. "He expects you soon."

All she does is nod, takes the bundle from him, and turn around to Hanka as the door closes again. She places the clothes carefully atop the little wooden table tucked into the corner and picks up the first big piece. Neither Basia nor Hanka can tell if they're looking at dark green shirts that are too big or dark green dresses that are too small with rounded necklines. Hanka doesn't recognize them at all as Kler garb. In fact, she doesn't know many people to have had spare clothing lying around in any town.

Basia flips the garment front, back, and inside out. "I could go without my armor for a single meal."

Hanka nods as she splashes water on her legs, rinsing the remaining cleanser. "I wish we could stay in these baths a little longer."

"If I were less cautious, I'd agree with you." She pats down her naked skin with the towel before throwing the dress over her head. It falls along her hardened curves, coming up high along her thighs. The tight sleeves tear when she moves her arms.

She laughs. It's the brightest sound Hanka has ever heard.

Still amused, she takes the socks and rolls them up. Because of the thickness of Basia's legs, the socks don't go up much higher than her knees.

It's fascinating to Hanka how different clothes can be completely changed by the frame upon which they lay. It makes her excited to get dressed, a feeling she cannot say she's experienced before. Every bit of clothing she has ever worn had been practical or rags, discarded from priests who have passed or whose garments far outlived their needs. A dress all her own is an unexpected luxury.

Once dried, she approaches Basia, who hands her the other garment. Hanka doesn't bother turning around when she lets the towel fall. The soft cotton caresses her skin, hanging loose like a frock. She swims in it, unlike Basia. The socks also climb up to her thighs.

They are less a matching pair and more a fitting one.

"I like how that looks on you," Basia says, smirking.

"Thank you." The phrase comes out a timid peep. "Do you think that when the lights come back, this is how comfortable we can be at all times or…" It sounds stupid to hope for peace and serenity. What the Kler had done to the world was destructive, but who knows that the return of the lights won't mete out equal violence.

"I think so," Basia says. She takes Hanka's hand in hers. "There might be more monsters, but at least people will be able to wander wherever they wish. I hope it means the end of the exile. Not that the Kolebka has much to offer the technomancers, but. It's a nice thought."

Hanka agrees. She wonders if she'll be hunted as one of those monsters, even though she never consented to being the creature she is.

They put on the matching slippers and open the door. The servant waits for them, and they follow their escort through the warmly lit halls of the Mistrz's Estate. It reminds Hanka of a more decorated Tawerna. While the vases and sconces show cracks from the skirmish, it indicates a level of care to the residence that simply had not been found where she last lived. The space feels lived in, with life's echoes etched into the frayed carpet, the scuff marks on the hardwood floor, and the dents in the walls. There are fewer stairs because the entire residence does not need to house every person who lives and works within it. There are dedicated spaces for dedicated people.

Hanka finds charm in it.

The servant opens the double doors at the end of a long hall, addressing them as "intruders" when announcing to the Mistrz that they have arrived. The scent of warm, buttery bread and stewed vegetables braised in unctuous broth fills her nose. Hanka's mouth waters immediately. It's like she's never eaten.

The Mistrz sits at the head of the wide table with table setting put out for his two guests. While they bathed, he cleaned up as well. His hood is gone, revealing yellow hair that sticks close to his scalp, still damp from the wash. The blood cleared off his face shows constellations of brown freckles dappled across his nose. He is handsome in the way his robe parts to reveal a hairy chest, breasts hidden by thick, luxurious fabric. It's the kind of softness that begs to be touched.

Hanka and Basia both keep their hands at their side as they join him for dinner.

"I hope you found the Mistrz's communal baths to your liking," he says, reaching for the tarnished goblet in front of him. He takes a loud sip. "It's been a long series of events, pardon if I am too quick to make myself comfortable." He gestures towards the servant. "Leave us."

The servant nods their head and exits the room, leaving the three of them alone with the roaring hearth behind the Baśni Mistrz.

It's just three of them. Hanka isn't one to lead conversations, and Basia seems to be reticent as well.

The Mistrz does it for them. "Please eat, I will not have my guests starve. Who do you think I am? The Kler?" He darts his eyes between them, waiting for them to reach for their spoons.

Hanka simply looks down at the reddish brown stew with scant greens dotting its surface. She reaches for her silverware, keeping her injured and strange left hand in her lap, beneath the table's lip, away from the Mistrz's gaze.

The soup tastes like liquid comfort, heavy and meaty with a texture that begs to be felt with all parts of her mouth. Spices she cannot identify prick at the corners of her tongue. Salt puckers her gums, begging to be chased down by a swig of water or the carmine alcohol sitting in her own goblet. She sips both. Refreshed. Welcomed.

"Oh, before I begin, perhaps some introductions are in order, I apologize for my rudeness." He tips his cup to Basia. "You first, technomancer. Who are you and how did you make your way back to the Kolebka?"

Basia exhales from her nose as she pats her lips dry with the brown kerchief before her. "My name is Basia, panie, and I came in from the lands beyond in a fellowship on a mission: discover why eliminating the constructs beyond the Kolebka did not bring the Nadziemscy back." Hearing Basia respectfully refer to the Mistrz as panie should not be so surprising, but it is the first Hanka has seen of her showing deference.

"So you mentioned. But why your fellowship? Why now?"

She pauses to drink, then answers, "The technomancers worked together to slaughter the remaining constructs. Some were decommissioned and repurposed for other technology, but otherwise, they are no longer a problem. We fulfilled our end of the pact. Then we waited. And waited." She takes another sip. "And waited until it was clear that the stars, the moons, and the sun weren't coming back. So, we took matters into our own hands."

"I see...something, however, tells me that this one—" The Mistrz indicates with Hanka with his drink. "Was not part of the fellowship. At least, I have never heard of any technomancer with such beastly eyes before."

He's the first one to have ever been so blunt about Hanka's bright blue eyes with their slit pupils. Instead of shying away, she turns her gaze to him. "That's because I'm not a technomancer. I'm from the Kolebka."

"But you're not from Stara Baśń either. That I can tell you for certain. It's not just your eyes, it's the absolute state in which both of you wandered here. You could have used the bridge."

Hanka raises a brow. "The bridge from which there are bodies hanging? The bridge cut off from the Droga?"

The Mistrz seems unbothered by this. "I suppose that might deter travel into the town, but unless you were a priest, there's nothing to worry about."

"Your guards arrested us upon our entry." Basia states it plainly. Hanka sees the way her shoulders tense. Hanka doesn't have the same instinct for fighting. She kicks her feet beneath the table, hoping to nudge Basia, but her legs don't quite reach.

"Chaos breeds paranoia, I apologize. I can tell you all about it, if you'd like." The way his voice lifts suggests a levity that should be reserved for ploys less blood-soaked.

Hanka leans forward. "Yes, please tell us all about this chaos you caused."

"Excellent, I can start yammering now." He takes a big spoonful of stew and takes his time easing it down his throat. With a satisfied sigh, he leans back to sip his cordial. "You two picked a strange time to infiltrate the Baśń. You're probably looking for some insight on all the bodies, on the pyres littering the streets. You want to know about the blood." Basia bobs her head as she eats. Hanka simply keeps her eyes on him as he talks. "If you want to assign blame, it should fall on the Kler, after all, they're the ones in charge of the world. Any ill that befalls us or them is their own fault." Another sip. "See, I had served the Kler as an acolyte, hoping to become a priest myself. At least, it's what I thought I wanted. It so happens that I didn't have the faith to continue on the practice of magic and conjunction with the night. The ability to cast left me a while ago."

Hanka does not see the miasma hovering around the Mistrz. In fact, her own is also faint, despite the harm she brought onto herself.

"During that uselessness, I made myself inquisitive, under the false notion that if I learned all I could about the Kler, my faith will be renewed. After all, it was the power I wanted more than I wanted the belief. The Kler attracts some intense believers, and I simply didn't have the right disposition for it."

"So, you set the Kler on fire and wreaked havoc on the Baśń out of listlessness?" Basia asks, raising a dark brow.

"I'm getting there. During the idle times when I should not have been wandering the Kler's complexes, I came across journals and manuscripts written in a script they only teach to the priests. They were about the 'maintenance' of the world." His mouth creases as he says it. "Maintenance is a strange word to use for something that's supposed to be a natural phenomenon."

Hanka tries to keep her face steady, but her eyes widen. It shocks her that someone so loosely affiliated with the Kler would have enough knowledge to uncover the truth of what they did to the world. She has no idea what the selection process is for new priests, but even given her own complicated relationship to her makers, she doesn't think there's any room for acolytes to disagree with their leaders or condemn the actions of their founders. Especially not in their stronghold where the entire populace is under their thumb.

"Because it isn't natural." He spits out each syllable. "I never thought the Kler would be the source of the darkness, and yet they kept records of it. If you had lived in the Baśń, you'd know how miserable the ceaseless night made our people. Aimless, listless, just passing on from ceremony to ceremony. Perhaps having children. Perhaps not. Stagnant." He leans forward, triumphant. "You cannot believe my immense joy to learn that there were so many others who were sick of it as well."

"You staged a rebellion," says Basia.

"On the contrary—the rebellion staged itself." He takes a drink. "The lights of Stara Baśń went out. The stars returned and—" The Baśńi Mistrz clicks his tongue. "The Baśń plunged into darkness. The Kler could not fix it. So, we fixed the Kler."

"Where'd you get weaponry from?" Hanka assumes that the Kler kept their swords and axes and other items with which they initially hunted the construct under the tightest of locks with the most hidden of keys.

"Any tool can become a weapon, if raised with the right sort of anger."

Hanka shivers. She regrets never thinking that the regular human populace would never fight back. It's the same assumption the Kler operated under, and it terrifies her how much they miscalculated.

"I have as much reason to hate the Kler as much as you do, Baśńi Mistrz," Basia drinks the clear water. "But the technomancers never had any interest in eliminating them."

"See, that might be because you didn't have to live under their lies. The terror of watching your loved ones be taken by their guard just for even complaining about the state of their stagnant lives. Some expressed a desire to leave Stara Baśń, and the Kler wasn't even allowing that. It didn't matter if the Mistrz granted permission; the role is just another tool of their dominance. Until that dominance wavered, of course."

"I haven't met a priest I haven't wanted to kill yet, so I perhaps somewhat understand your point of view." Basia looks to Hanka and winks. "The kind of vengeance we are looking for is the kind that undoes their mass manipulation."

The Mistrz turns to Basia. "If you are looking for...another Strażnik, what are you doing here?"

Basia shrugs. "We don't know where another Strażnik is. Gwiedzna Wieża had nothing for us. There weren't even people. We wanted to see if civilization had anything to offer."

"And civilization might." The Mistrz rises from the table. "Sit and eat up. I'm going to rest, and we shall reconnect at a later time. My servants will be waiting to escort you to where we dropped off your belongings. Smacznego." He takes his goblet with him but leaves behind his half-eaten meal.

Both of them sigh loudly when the door finally shuts behind the Mistrz and his servant. It relieves Hanka that the Baśni Mistrz dropped the entire question of who she is. The relief almost brings tears to her eyes because sooner rather than later, she will need to tell Basia about her inhumanity and about the reasons why she had to run away from the Katedra, even though she somehow had no inkling that the rest of humanity might also be done with the darkness.

CHAPTER SEVEN

CONSTRUCTS

JITKA: POLITICS HAD NO PLACE IN THE WILD SPACES WHERE BEASTS ROAM

THE SERVANT CALLED THIS a guest room, likely a relic from the time before the Zaćmienie when people would have guests and travelers wandering from across the Kolebka, even welcomed from the land beyond. The one word Basia can find for it is plush. Layers of carpets and furs cover the entire floor. Tapestries hang from the walls not in a way that suggests storage, but in an artful arrangement that seems to tell the story of a hunt. Basia doesn't know any Kolebskie stories or what parables the Kler might use to justify the all-consuming darkness, But the fact that she cannot even assign the stars, the moons, and the sun to the different small animals running around and dancing within each piece troubles her. She wants to call it a hunt, but there's no blood or weaponry, but the frenetic way the threads tangle over each other suggest some kind of violence.

Fiber arts are not for her to understand or decipher.

The weariness in her bones pulls her to the four-poster bed sized more for a small family than a pair of women coming in from the wrong side of Stara Baśń's many tiers. Billowy duvets give way to her sore muscles and full stomach. Basia wedges her face between two pillows, and if she closes her eyes for too long, she will fall asleep. She can't remember the last time sleep was allowed to have such a hold on her.

Dinner wasn't particularly heavy or indulgent, but it was warm and a meal. She wishes she could also touch Hanka, feel the coolness of her skin against her warm body, but the bard is too busy fussing over the candles and lanterns lit by more conventional flame.

When her eyes flutter shut, they don't stay that way for long. Hanka's scream yanks her out of that liminal space on the verge of sleep. She points to the window overlooking the opposite side of the town. A large metallic bird barrels towards their room. The stars twinkle outside, and Basia is so frustrated that she didn't consider that those soft, twinkling lights might be able to reawaken anything left hibernating in the Kolebka. The bird glows bright blue, not the cozy orange or alert white that accompanies the colors of the technomancer constructs—something about it feels wrong, especially the way it has no regard for its form or its function as it crashes into the window. The thick glass does not shatter.

Hanka jolts, but Basia stares at it. This wasn't made by her people.

Deterred, the construct flies back, veers around. An immense sense of responsibility seizes Basia's heart. A shirt and some socks are not armor. The constructs are likely after Hanka, and it's her role to protect her. It's up to her to investigate this strange piece of violent technology.

"Stay here," she yells to Hanka as she gets her boots back on and retrieves her sword. As long as the bard hides inside this room, she'll be safe. It's what Basia wants to believe.

Word must have spread about the construct in Stara Baśń because as Basia runs through the halls, the servants and the Mistrz's allies all shout orders at each other to stay inside. One of them—a stooped older woman who herself struggles to teeter down the steps—reaches for Basia as she makes her way down. She ducks under her arm. Another servant attempts to grab her. Why they would attempt stopping a bitch with a sword is beyond her.

She kicks the front door open to the hexagonal plaza at the center of which is a wide pool of stagnant water. Smoldering piles of ash and bone dot the corners. Whizzing and screeching, the construct flies in frenetic circles overhead, turning its flapping, cape-like wings in careful angles to avoid getting caught on the dimmed lanterns. The only light helping her see the full space still belongs to the pyres of dispatched priests.

At least they're good for something.

No one else needs to get hurt as long as she can fight. With a whisper and tweak of rozpalić, her sword engulfs in flames. She runs out, waving her sword around like a flagpole to get the construct's attention. This noise interrupts its flight pattern. It freezes in midair, shining eyes searching for her. It locks on and dives towards her, metal joints grinding as it builds up momentum by spiraling towards the earth. Its folded wings trail behind like ribbons. Its beak points directly at her, a straight pike built to pierce. Her flesh is weaker than a window, and there is little room for error.

Basia takes a step back then raises her sword in an elegant arch pointing where the construct intends to skewer her. Dropping her arms at the last moment, the blade connects with its cone-shaped head, crunching through metal. Oil and the facsimile of blood fizzle against her flames. Her weapon crunches into the chassis of its skull.

The construct stabs into the ground instead, its body flipping like an overturned table. She steps to the side, evading the trajectory of its crash. It tears through the plaza. Shards of stone fly up in its wake. As it slides into the pool's side, the gears within it whir to a halt. The lights glowing from inside its chest dim. Silence follows.

Even simple battles like this make her sweaty and take the breath from her lungs. She douses the fire on her sword when she hears clapping from behind her.

"That was an incredible display, technomancer," the Mistrz says. He still isn't fully dressed after dinner, having left the Estate in his own black slippers embroidered with stars that glitter in the Estate's pale lights.

"My name is Basia," she spits out.

"*Basia*," he corrects himself. "I suppose the return of the lights do pose a problem with constructs. It's so funny to me, the Kler said they had your people eliminate all the constructs from the Kolebka. So, what's this about?"

It's the question her fellowship sought to answer. "See, I thought it was just Strażnicy." But no, it seems there are far more constructs than they initially considered. But this thing cannot be a technomancer construct, not with its design and the way it fizzles and shines. Could it be possible that the Kler decided to make their own constructs out of the night-kissed magic? The Strażnicy are still infused with celestial light; Basia recognized the one in the Gwiedzna Wieża as her people's own make. These new creatures mean that the Kler is making constructs of their own, thus going back on their agreement with the technomancers to rid the world of their sun-embraced progenitors. Darkness should not beget more darkness. If such a thing were possible, the Kler's control would have no bounds, and there would be no consequences for what they did to the world.

Basia and the Mistrz stand in silence while each of them considers what to say to the other. No one rushes out to meet them, which Basia would find strange if not for the fact that the darkness keeps the people inside. Now there are constructs to contend with? She would be staying within the confines of a decaying apartment as well.

"It seems, to me, the people still have much reason to fear the outside," the Mistrz says. "Perhaps you brought it with you?"

She glares at him. "If that construct were mine, it would have come in with us. I should have used it for conquest or…" The words stop. She has never heard of the constructs being used for battle or war, not since before the Zaćmienie. Someone else in the Kolebka might have had the imagination, but she has never been an engineer. "It's not ours. I'd like to study it. Is there anything resembling a lab in the Estate?" She spits out a thick glob of saliva. "Or anywhere that would fit that thing."

The construct she just felled is an imitation one of the smaller designs that the technomancers who kept the art of creature construction alive outside the Kolebka. It's not something Basia had ever studied or had any interest in. But she knows how constructs are supposed to work. They don't attack technomancers. They serve a function: defending against night-kissed beasts and whatever else is programmed as an enemy.

Rage blossoms within her chest at the notion that the Kler would turn stolen constructs against their creators. Everything the Kler touches with their magical cleverness turns to ruin. Even outside the Kolebka, between the fellowship, there was little talk of what happened during the battles and skirmishes of the Zaćmienie. Basia doesn't know how she would have ended up at its onset, but if she had survived the beginning, she knows one thing now: there'd be a much longer trail of bodies tailing behind her.

"I actually haven't done that much investigating, but I don't think anyone has the strength to lift that thing. I surely don't." The Mistrz scratches his chin with a nail. "What do you need to examine it?"

Hanka. She needs Hanka to examine it. "Can you get the bard from our room? It's safe now, and I don't want her to worry."

"If I weren't so observant, I'd say you have a soft spot for her." Basia whips her head up to stare at the Baśni Mistrz, who guffaws at her in response. "You're not so mysterious, Basia. But I will acquiesce." He returns indoors, perhaps to get Hanka, leaving Basia alone.

Her face burns from exertion and her own earnestness. Had she been that lonely this entire excursion within the Kolebka that she fell so hard and so easily? She doesn't know exactly what Hanka *is.* Not a technomancer. Not a priest. Not even human. Eating the flesh of a night-kissed beast flesh had not even occurred to Basia, not even the few times hunger proved a greater enemy than the dangers wandering these darkened lands. Her own abilities came from her own strength and innovations that preceded her, but Hanka's come from something else entirely.

She shakes her head as if she had just splashed water on it and goes over to the fallen construct. It's not so scary up close. It's also not right, the body made of tarnished gray metal instead of the gold gleam of the ones made by the technomancers. She crouches before the bird, running her fingers over the pocked, tarnished surface. The metal gleams silver with many uneven edges hastily soldered together, and comes to a conclusion.

This is a shoddily cobbled together replacement for the Strażnik she has already destroyed.

The rage inside her has her gritting her teeth. She almost wants to ask Hanka if she knows where the Kler does their experimentation. Nothing would bring her greater pleasure than to destroy it. Put an end to all of their projects and products.

She gently lays her sword on the ground before running her fingers along the bird's wings. They aren't strong enough to ever transport items or people, meaning this a combat item, created to ensure that the night stays eternal. She would be impressed if it wasn't an abomination.

"Basia!" Hanka calls to her as she jogs down the steps. She's half-dressed in clothing she must have scavenged from the bedroom. "What is this?"

"It *looks* like a construct, but it's not one made by technomancers. Is there anything you can do to—"

As she speaks, Hanka reaches for the broken pipe sticking out from the construct's side from which the oil leaks. It sluices onto her fingers, staining them with blue gray liquid. Without prompting, she brings it to her lips, shuddering as she gives it a taste. Then doesn't anything as she licks each of her fingers, fellating them to cleanliness.

When she doesn't say anything after smacking her lips together, Basia asks, "Well?"

Hanka frowns. "This tastes exactly like the night. I don't think that's what constructs are supposed to taste like."

Basia groans, wincing. "Please don't tell me you've tasted *other* constructs."

"Sometimes my curiosity gets the best of me. And there were leaks all the time in Tawerna, but I wasn't a mechanic." Hanka is so lucky she is as charming as she is because otherwise, Basia might consider terminating their companionship.

Well, that, and also her curiosity for the hidden knowledge that Hanka hasn't shared the source of yet. And the ability to fend off night-kissed beasts and other constructs.

"So, wanderers," the Baśni Mistrz asks, joining them in the plaza. "Why is there a construct in my town newly liberated from the Kler?"

"This is something new. Something made by the Kler to keep people like me out." It's the only answer Basia can give with any certainty.

"Fascinating." The Mistrz sounds less interested than this single word implies. "Of course, if you are a technomancer, you would have knowledge of proper constructs." His interest waxes as he continues, "Perhaps you two can discover what doused the Baśni lights. There's no point in liberating the people from the Kler if now we have new monsters and more darkness to deal with."

"I don't want hospitality." Basia crouches to pick up her sword. "If you want my help, what we need is to know the locations of the last two Strażnicy. I won't take anything else."

He smirks. "I almost expected you to point that sword at me. No matter. Please return to your rooms, make yourselves comfortable. I'll escort you to the archives and ensure those loyal to me are at your disposal. We wouldn't want you losing to your base needs while trying to uncover secrets the Kler hoped no one would reveal to the rest of the populace."

Basia would call it a kindness, but it's a simple exchange of services. She looks at Hanka. The bard just nods at her.

"We have an accord."

WHEN THE HEAVY WOODEN door opens to reveal the interior of the archives, it's then Hanka realizes that this space is absolutely nothing like the Kler's research facilities in the Katedra. For one, the walls are more windows than shelving. Tables line the center like a banquet hall. Whoever had been in that facility left in a haste; papers litter the rolling trays and books lay open where someone had been interrupted in their reading. Statues of priests mark off each section, the inscriptions on their books indicating the subject matter found within each row.

Patryk had taught her the Kler's glyphs and how to read them. She wonders if the Baśń Mistrz had gotten a similar level of education.

He guides them to a section where the books are particularly disheveled, half of them open in haphazard piles all around. "All right, this entire facility is yours. Here is where I started my discoveries. I'm not sure how helpful it will be to your end of the bargain, but I figure I offer them to you. Happy reading."

The Baśń Mistrz departs with the pair of servants who leave behind pitchers of water and stewed fruits. Hanka pinches some of the dripping fruit slices and slurps them up before taking a lap around the room. Her footfalls slowly echo against the floor.

Meanwhile, there's a charm to the witch's diligence, for Basia brought her sword and her backpack, and she kneels, riffling through her bag for her notebooks. But the handful of notebooks that come out cannot be all that makes the backpack so heavy. If Hanka didn't know Basia, she would snoop, take advantage of the ways she can see in the darkness and examine what's in there. Just as she must tell Basia her own truths, she also has a feeling that there will come a time when Basia tells her more of the fellowship and the journey to the Kolebka.

"So, here's the thing," Basia says as she sits down at one of the tall wooden chairs. "I'm not a construct builder. I cannot explain why the lights went out. I cannot explain the construct in the town. All the information we have to find the Strażnicy must be here. Why don't we just take it and leave?"

Hanka stops and tilts her head at Basia. "Isn't that a bit cruel?"

"It's a problem with the Kler. The towns won't need the lights if we bring the moons and the sun back."

Hanka exhales, pursing her lips. It's times like this when she wishes she knew slightly more about any mechanical thing. In Tawerna, when leaks had happened in the town itself, she had been of some use, but she had never been allowed deeper into the town's bowels. Where the lights and the heat came from were a total mystery to her. How energy is converted and used is a study only for the priests who prepared the Mistrzowie, a process completely hidden away from even most of the Kler.

"I can't prove that you're wrong," is what Hanka eventually says. "But you're a technomancer, perhaps you can help? Something must have gone wrong with Stara Baśń's mechanism."

"Not my problem."

"It might become a problem if the Kler comes to fix it themselves. I don't want to be here when that happens."

"Then those other constructs can take care of them. It isn't our fault that their solutions to making sure the towns survive the darkness are less than permanent."

Hanka makes her way back and kneels beside her. "It would be *our* fault, though. We're the only ones hunting Strażnicy. Imagine if we free the sun next. The entire Kolebka is going to fall to ruin and..." Hanka swallows down the thickness in her throat. Her skin warms and her joints creak with the tightness that nearly rooted her to her own ruin back in the Katedra, when had she activated one of the constructs she wasn't supposed to even know about. Out in the plaza, she had recognized the flavor immediately. This construct had tasted the same. "There will be nowhere else to run."

Her voice is cracking, and her eyes burn. She didn't ask to be a night-kissed beast who must also be human. Hanka closes her eyes, hearing the scrape of the chair against the floor. Hands touch her shoulders, and her lids flutter open. Basia's face is soft, concerned. Not pitying, but gentle.

Basia says, not unkindly, "I would say you don't have to tell me anything, Hanka. But if this secrecy is going to keep us from defeating the Strażnicy, I'll have to wrench it from you, and I really don't want to do that."

"All right. Can I have a seat next to you?"

"Of course." None of the chairs have armrests, so Basia picks them up, lining three side by side so they can form a kind of bench. The cushions are folded blankets. She unfolds them, smoothing them out to create a single piece to sit on. "This might not be the most comfortable, but I don't want to sit across from you like we're having some kind of conference. We've been through too much for such formality."

Hanka almost wants to sit in her lap so she at least has somewhere to cry when she inevitably starts weeping because she's been so alone for so long. Instead, they sit beside each other. Basia hangs her arm over the headrest and rests her chin in the crook of her elbow. She looks lethargic and cozy in the over-sized knit sweater that swallows her body. Hanka wishes she could just look at her instead of having to divulge her past. But, as far as she knows, Basia has shared her full story. It's time for Hanka to reciprocate.

She sits cross-legged in the comfortable dress the Mistrz had given them for dinner, resting her hands where the hem makes a tent between her legs. Preserving whatever modesty she has left shouldn't matter at this point.

For so many years, Hanka has isolated because she isn't human, sequestering her truth because it will spell her ruin. There's been enough of secrecy. "I'm not a priest. I'm not a technomancer. But I only look human. The truth is, I'm a night-kissed beast." A weight lifts from her chest as she finally says it. "As if the eyes didn't make it obvious."

Basia nods, understanding. She's not one for talking to encourage the other person to continue speaking, and for that, Hanka is grateful. The stillness of Basia's face concerns her. It makes her worry that perhaps this truth is something she should have kept secret, that she should have let the witch believe whatever she likes about Hanka. The lie would have been difficult to uphold and even as she prepares to tell her story, it surprises Hanka how easily the words tumble out.

"Stara Baśń is where the Kler trains priests. Katedra Wieszczów is where the Kler raises its night-kissed beasts. It's where the darkness started. I don't know what version of the Zaćmienie the technomancers teach, but what I came to learn was this: the constructs had gone wild, achieving a sentience that should not have been possible. The first priests bred creatures with the opposite magic to fight them, which led to a revolution that resulted in thousands of constructs dead, but thousands more running amok. The primordial Kler came into power and then forced all the technomancers out, all while starting the Wieczna Noc."

"That is the version I've been taught as well."

"Within the many, many facilities at the Katedra, they still breed more night-kissed beasts. There aren't many laypeople in the Katedra because the lie is that the night-kissed beasts are natural, not made."

"Oh, fuck off." Basia chews her bottom lip. "My apologies, the lies simply never end."

Hanka understands the anger. It might be the only thing she understands out of everything the Kler brought together. "It's mostly to keep people off the Droga, scared to explore the Kolebka or the lands beyond. But then a curious thing happened in one brood: twins had been born. Patryk and I came out of the incubating beast's cloaca not in eggs like the rest of the beasts, but wrapped in film. The priests called us a miracle.

And I guess we were. Humans made of night's kiss rather than mere humans who can harness it. They didn't know what to do with us."

"How so?" Basia straightens.

"Night-kissed beasts are only animals, but we could understand the priests just fine, processed their words, so clearly we were more human than beast. We went from crawling to standing like the other Kler-born children. So, they had us with them until they found we didn't develop like our human peers. Where they had to be taught their magic, we just used it naturally. The priests had us join the Kler much younger than the other acolytes. There was jealousy there, I think. But of course, they expected us to be loyal. The Kler was our family—our parents—after all. But then, much like the Baśni Mistrz, I got curious."

She lets the words wash over Basia for a few breaths. Hanka fondly remembers the unfettered way they of the twin beasts had wandered around the Katedra. They needed to mingle among children to learn how to be human, because the Kler adults were not going to do that developing for them. By any measure, it was a largely happy childhood. Full of play, even though there were a few too many instances where their strange eyes frightened the other children. The abilities even more—they wielded night's kiss like the adults.

But that happiness had not lasted forever. Even now, to speak of it raises old fears. "The Kler had several projects. One of them involved trying to recreate the technology that keeps the world alight. Ways to push back against the darkness. But it involved the mutilation of beasts. They wanted me to be one of the prototypes. I got scared. I ran."

Basia takes a deep breath. "Is it that simple?"

"No." Sickness gathers in the back of her mouth. She remembers the metal. She remembers the screeching and the grinding of gears. The pain she had forgotten in her stomach and hips returns for the first time since the discovery. She squirms in her seat. "I wasn't the first one though. I tried to warn Patryk, but he didn't understand. He believes in the darkness. He's afraid of the constructs that the Kler had supposedly eliminated. He fears the light. As beasts, it's our duty to uphold the Wieczna Noc. I wanted none of it. So, I ran, but not before freeing all the constructs I could find."

"Did any of them look like the thing that attacked our room?"

Hanka shakes her head. "It's been so long since I'd run. I've no doubt they figured it out and replaced the ones they lost."

It would hurt her—it does hurt her—to think that Patryk stayed to aid in that research, that torture. The harm done to their brethren is something that should have been too much to endure. But perhaps that sensitivity and softness had been a failure in Hanka's design.

Basia bites down on one of her knuckles. "If they're going to make night-kissed constructs, they should start smaller. Like the lanterns across the Droga—those lamps are all miniatures, but those lights stay on."

"That might explain the purpose of the pilgrimages..." Hanka sighs. "How many of those sun-embraced constructs have been replaced by the night-kissed without anyone's knowledge?"

The witch shrugs. "How should I know? I'm convinced the Droga would set me aflame if I so much as dreamed going near it."

"I can't even say you'd be wrong for thinking that." Hanka groans. "I hate the idea of this darkness continuing."

Basia's next question is hard to hear. "And what about Patryk? How much of a threat is he? He was at Tawerna. He's a priest now, right?"

"Patryk loved the Kler. Maybe still does." Hanka licks her lips. "You know, I'm actually not sure. If he truly loved the Kler, he'd be in Stara Baśń, seeking us out."

"He might not have thought to check Stara Baśń."

The burning pyres all throughout Stara Baśń shine in Hanka's mind like a lantern. Fear crawls up her spine and leaves her lips in a shout. "He's not here!" She grabs the sides of her head, as if she can squeeze that terrible notion out of her mind.

Patryk might have let her go, but she holds no ill will against him. In fact, she harbors a resentment against him for not chasing after her. They could have survived in the Kolebka together, as twin beasts. Hanka doesn't know why the Kler didn't fight harder to get her back. Perhaps they didn't want to start a conflict with their towns. If both she and Patryk had escaped, perhaps the Kler would have chased them more.

But they were willing to bring fire to Tawerna to stop Basia. Had Hanka been too precious for them to perceive a threat? The only time she gave them something to fear was when she activated the constructs, and that had not been her own power.

Basia leans forward. "I'm not saying he is. You might have been able to sense him, right? If he was dead, you'd be in so much pain. Just like the other time."

Hanka didn't think Basia would have noticed. She thought the witch simply attributed her pain to having used magic, not to the strange connection Hanka shares with all her kin. There aren't any such echoes of pain anywhere in her body. The ones dispatched here had all been Kler. If there were beasts, she would know.

"You're right. I didn't think you'd notice."

"Please, I would've been killed far sooner if I noticed less." The smile Basia gives is weak. "I'm willing to do whatever it takes to keep the Kler away from us, even if it means investigating the mechanisms that should be keeping the lights going."

It warms Hanka's heart that they agree on this one thing.

Basia stands and cranes her neck to look around the archive. "So, where would information about the Strażnicy be?"

Hanka has never been in a Mistrz's study before, and the Baśńi Mistrz didn't seem familiar with the concept of the Strażnicy, which means that information cannot be in the books he left strewn about. She has no idea where to even look, but if she had to guess, it would be a hidden entrance to clandestine depths.

She takes a deep breath and gets off the seat. In the far side of the space, there is a desk like an altar flanked by two sets of short steps. The once-deep blues carpeting the floor are now pale gray, the threads worn and frayed from frequent pacing. Hanka crouches, touching the ground with her raw, night-kissed index finger, hoping for resonance, for the magic to sing to an echo. It's faint, the whisper of spells long-cast settling like dust. She follows it, crawling on her toes like a critter. It leads her up the steps and around to the middle of the desk. The seams of one cabinet shimmer with night's kiss.

Of course, Kler who weren't the ruling Mistrz would need to be able to find the doors to their own technology.

"Did you find anything?" Basia calls to her, keeping her distance.

"I think so…" Hanka runs her nascent digit along the seam. Night's kiss recognizes its own. The stone scrapes against itself as the doorway slides open.

The smell that blooms from the opening is sour and charred. Hanka gags. It is food gone bad and a hearth burnt to nothing. Abandoned.

Basia comes up behind her. "This entrance seems too small for anyone to use." She places her hands on the top of the altar.

Hanka hears the movement before Basia startles. The top pops open like a lid to a chest. Hanka steadies Basia as she wavers. They watch with wide eyes as the floor recedes to reveal steps descending into opaque darkness. Pricks like the twinkling stars illuminate the steps, their cold blue hue glowing with night's kiss.

"Can you see the lights?" Hanka asks.

Basia shakes her head.

Hanka grabs her hand. "If you follow my steps, I'll guide you."

Basia's pink lips quirk to a half-smile. "Wasn't that our agreement?"

It was. Tawerna seems so far away, however. And at least with finding the Gwiedzna Wieża, Hanka knew where to lead Basia. But now, all they have are the lights provided by those who created is this darkness. The only hope they have in each other, in their separate talents for observation. Basia doubts the next clue would come from the Kler itself, but she welcomes the surprise if it comes.

BASIA LEAVES HER SWORD behind—the light bathing the cluttered archives is of more use than having it illuminate these stairs that Hanka can see without the assistance. In fact, świecik might get in the way of that visibility. It's Hanka's ability to see night's kiss that got them this far. In spite of that ability, it's her lack of affinity or affiliation with the Kler that makes Basia feel somewhat safe around the bard.

By the time they reach the bottom, she's counted several hundred stairs. This gullet they entered reminds Basia of the first time she left for the Kolebka, of how darkness crawled along her skin without any nearby light to cast it away. Then, what had made the wilderness so frightening in those first wanderings was how much of it there was. Nothing should go on forever. The darkness is even worse now the walls are within arms' reach—In this tiny space, the endless bounds of darkness reach for her, and she can't do anything to shake it off except to walk deeper into its embrace. Her legs ache from the uncertainty, from the care with which she had to step, from her utter reliance on Hanka. It still feels too good to be true that she found a companion who can see in the dark, who can bear witness to night's kiss.

If Hanka hadn't been so sure-footed, if she hadn't been right with all her observations this entire journey so far, then Basia would have called it a farce. Or Basia would have waited for her to take a chance at her life, ending the fellowship of technomancers and condemning the world to the Kler's abyss.

But no such danger threatens Basia. Hanka has been true to her promise of guidance.

After they have caught their breath at the bottom of the stairs, Hanka lets out a loud exhale. The darkness swallows them both. There's no wind to help Basia measure the space around them.

"What is it? What do you see?" Basia keeps her voice low, barely above a murmur. She fears a den. She fears some creature made its nest here, and Hanka is here to deliver Basia as a last supper.

"What can *you* see?" Hanka replies.

"Nothing, I see nothing." She tries not to change her grip. Too tight would betray fear. To loosen it would suggest mistrust.

"There's...a construct. I don't—" The bard swallows loudly. "I'm not sure what I'm looking at, and I don't have anything with which to conjure a light."

"Can you take me to it?" If it's machinery, Basia can make do. These are the mechanisms of her people, after all.

Hanka's grip on her hand tightens as she gently pulls Basia through the cavern. Within a cistern is not how anything should be housed. It makes Basia sick—the constructs ran on several types of batteries and other innovations to manage the night, but they were never to be sequestered in pure darkness and especially not in air this heavy and dank. She doesn't care if it's in a diminished capacity. Even dregs deserve the same dignity as their complete counterparts.

Hanka yelps, which startles Basia.

"What is it?" she asks, keeping her jaw steady because they cannot both be afraid. One at a time or neither at all.

"It's so...wet? I don't think I've ever touched the miasma before." A pathetic whimpering groan leaves Hanka's mouth. "This is so unpleasant. Here, maybe you know what it is."

Before Basia can protest, Hanka yanks her hand forward. Basia's palm presses against metal so cold it burns. Unpleasant is too weak a word for the feeling. Fundamentally incorrect describes it better. Where her skin feels pain, her heart aches too. She's never felt this kind of connection to anything, let alone something automatic whose own search for autonomy and sentience made it a threat to the world around it. A threat so terrible that a Kler arose to put it down, lock it away.

The sensation that greets her palm isn't stickiness, just sadness and cold.

"I feel metal. This might be a construct." It's the only truth Basia can claim.

Hanka coughs, loudly. "The miasma is really bad. It's like excrement."

"What if you tried to burn it away?" Basia asks. She tries to think of how she would go about protecting herself and her gear from the world's wetness. Water dried off, faster by a fire. This texture unsettling Hanka, however, is something unseen.

"Maybe? I've only used night's kiss; I cannot claim any understanding of how it works." She winces. "I'm so sorry. Understanding is for the Kler, not for...well, the beasts."

Basia nods. It's similar with the technomancers. Some cast their magic for maintenance. Others push it to its limit, which is how the constructs used to power towns came into being at all. And then there's Basia who simply has her tools and nary a technical understanding of the mechanisms behind her trinkets and baubles. "Same for me with technomancy. All I've got are tools. If you lead me to the stairs, I think I can get my sword, and we'll figure something out."

She lets her lips spread into a smile; she knows Hanka can see it, even if Basia has no idea what expression the bard returns.

Hanka gently places her hands on Basia's shoulders and turns her around. The bard's foot nudges her ankle and she takes steps forward. The floor is solid between her feet; it's the fear of the dark that has her stepping unsteadily. But soon enough, she sees the faint glow of świecik from the bottom of the stairs.

"I can crawl up from here," Basia says. "I've moved in worse places."

The bard gives her shoulders a squeeze. "I'll stay here and try to figure out...whatever that is."

Basia doesn't bother looking over her shoulders, climbing instead. Her steps are slow, measured, making sure the tips of her boots hit the lip of the step in front of her before ascending the next one. It's slow going, but relief smothers her when she returns to the archives and only now does she think to have taken one of the lanterns with them on the first descent. Now, though, something tells her natural light won't suffice. They need something stronger. She should have brought her blade, and świecik, with her when they entered the depths.

The trust she had in Hanka leading them somewhere that poses no immediate threat clouded her judgment.

She wraps her hand around her sword's hilt, lifting it from beside the altar, the bright light of świecik crawling up the metal, turning the steel itself into its own kind of torch. Under her light as she descends, the stone steps are all sable, a worn surface pocked from years of use, scarred from people bringing machinery up and down.

When Basia reaches the bottom, Hanka turns her head to look at the brightness she has brought with her. She shields her eyes with splayed fingers.

"It's burning away the miasma," she shouts. "Come closer!"

Basia walks, her feet echoing against the unused, glazed floor. Her sword's fire reflects off the smooth surface, making świecik's light seem larger than it actually is. Instead of the softly glowing arch of her blade, there is a raging inferno. The stone of the cavern captures the heat, beading sweat along Basia's cheeks and forehead. It doesn't cause discomfort—it's only now she realizes just how cold Stara Baśń has been without the support of a construct providing light or radiating heat throughout the town. The pyres of the burning Kler can only burn so long. When they go out, the only fire left will be the revenge burning in the hearts of the people of Stara Baśń. That fire won't create heat or light, though; it only maintains the will to keep on going.

As świecik's glow peels apart the dark, Basia drops her sword, grief gripping her chest.

Basia recognizes the machinery. Like most of the stationary constructs, it has a body engineered for specific functionality. Wires and tubes criss-cross against its smooth metal, running along divots and tracks. Shadows smother and scar the construct, choking it. Basia might not see the miasma, but the faint darkness denting and scarring the metal is enough evidence of waste allowed to proliferate. In the lands beyond the Kolebka, there was always a technomancer around to burn away the waste.

If she were in charge of the Kler, she would have taught the Mistrzowie the spells, just like how Hanka seems to have taught herself how to manipulate technomancy.

But this construct had been left to rot. Technology doesn't work indefinitely. There will always need to be someone around to care for it.

Not the Kler though. They wanted power, not comfort. This is the world they left everyone because they were afraid of sentient constructs, letting even their diminished forms fall into ruin while they failed to learn the lifespan of these once-living beings. The technomancers might have been wrong in letting their creations run amok but imprisoning them in these grottoes is not the answer either.

Whirring like a roar sends a shock through them. Basia jogs over and catches Hanka as she staggers backward, uneven on her feet. Triggered by świecik's magic, lights come on along where the wall and the ceiling meets. Gold bathes the room in heat, with the warmth to follow soon.

There's no comfort in the dispelling darkness. The Kler let that construct fall to ruin, and Stara Baśń with it.

"Are you all right?" Hanka asks.

Basia lets out a sharp grunt through clenched teeth. "I hate them, Hanka, I hate the Kler so much." The words tremble as they tumble from her lips. "That's not supposed to happen, the constructs aren't supposed to be touched by darkness. They're supposed to be tended."

It's the same anger she felt when she realized that the Strażnik Astralny didn't have a name. It's the same anger she felt when the Droga itself betrayed her and her fellowship. It's all rage, and she knows she has to keep her focus on eliminating the other Strażnicy. But this desire for vengeance runs deep. There is a part of her that asks, why not kill the Kler first and bring the light back later?

Bathed in reanimated light, Stara Baśń's controlling construct has a visage like a sun covered in eyes. It hangs close to the ceiling, each of the metal eyes glowing as power runs through it. If Basia were the sentimental type, she would it imagine it smiling and thanking her for bringing it back to life. Such gratitude is unearned—soon enough it will get swallowed up by night through the Kler's neglect. Neither Basia nor any other technomancer will be around to clean it, to keep its furnace burning and its light shining.

Hanka says, "Maybe we can teach the Mistrz how to do this cleaning. If all it takes is some—"

Basia glares back. "If he is Kler-trained, he knows night's kiss, not technomancy. To wield both is rare." Hanka seems unaware of how unique she is, a facility for both shadow and light Basia has never seen in another. It should be enough to anger one or both of them.

Hanka's expression, however, remains soft. It remains hopeful and kind. The fact that knowing what the Kler wanted to do to her did not harden her edges makes Basia both concerned and jealous. "If the darkness can be taught, so can the light."

"I'm not a teacher!" Basia only wants to bring the light back to the world so none of this nonsense has any hope of continuing.

"You don't have to be." Hanka gently holds Basia's elbows and helps her back on her feet. "If the Baśni Mistrz understood enough to learn the truth, then he can figure out how to make magic happen. It's a skill, just like any other."

If only that were true; not even every child born to a technomancer has the affinity for the sun's embrace. Not all of them are touched by it, but technomancy isn't just the magic. There's engineering and other skills and practices essential for keeping things in working order. Everyone can have a role. It's the Kler's folly for thinking they're the only ones deserving of power.

In a way, Hanka is right, and she's the only one who resents the Kler in the same way Basia does in the entire Kolebka. She refuses to continue alone, and she won't push away her sole ally now. "I suppose that is true. I apologize, just seeing this..." Basia can't find the right word. "It's alive now, I think."

They both look upon the construct and its spinning gears and the chains clicking from one tooth to the next. Plumes of other smoke belch from rustier sections, but it's the remnants of night's kiss burned away by the light releasing.

"I'd say so," the bard says. "Now that that's dealt with, we have a Strażnik to find."

With her sword in hand and Hanka's arm around her waist, Basia takes them both back to the stairway and up into the archive. Their work is done, but now they need to find their reward.

CHAPTER EIGHT

DEPARTURES

HENIEK: EVEN THE DROGA COULDN'T BE TOO BRIGHT FOR HIM

IN THE ARCHIVE, THEY sit quietly together, searching through the documents and trying to find the location of the next Strażnik. Basia's silence is not a comforting thing to Hanka. In fact, it makes her worry. She should be happy that she got to bring not one by two lights back to the Kolebka. Sure, one is grander, but the other means that Stara Baśń is fully freed from the Kler. One stronghold no longer belongs to them; it belongs to the people. Should they want it back, they will need to fight for their influence to be returned to them, much like how they took control of this world so long ago.

Hanka isn't sure how many more cities there are to fall, and she doesn't want to witness that violent destruction herself. At the same time, she hates how much comfort it brings her that it's not just her and Basia fighting back against this ceaseless darkness. The enlightenment of its wrongness is no longer her own. There are others.

If only people other than the Kler knew where the Strażnicy were, then that would be a boon to freeing the world from this abyssal tyranny.

The Kler's texts are incomprehensible, even beyond the fact that Hanka has found she's somewhat lost the ability to read their text. There was a time when she could, having stolen it from the Katedra. Perhaps, if she hadn't run off scared because the Kler also wanted her as a broodmother, she could have discovered more. If only she could have practiced, but in Tawerna, the language of the Kler had been hidden away in in the Mistrz's quarters, to stop the laypeople from learning the failing truth of the Kolebka.

There are enough illustrations in each of the books and ledgers that perhaps someone who cannot decipher the words labeling arrows and circles can still figure out what it is they read. Hanka has the benefit of all the knowledge her sneaking around the Katedra brought her. Instead, she's tucked away in the Kler's stronghold of training, trying to learn the rest of what she doesn't know.

It's been hours since they last spoke, and Hanka hates the silence. In Tawerna, there had at least always been a band playing their music. Since Hanka is not here as entertainment and making Basia do all the research herself would be unfair, she left her balalaika behind in the bedroom. She didn't want to distract. Whistling or humming might bring more annoyance than comfort, and Basia's expression is all frustration and grinding teeth. Something is wrong, but Hanka wants to give Basia time. If she wants to share that with Hanka, she can.

When she finishes the pitcher of water the Mistrz left for them, she says, "Do you want me to go to the Baśni Mistrz and ask for more?"

Basia swallows hard, then looks up from her reading at Hanka. Her eyes are red and glassy. "I want to quit."

"What?" She should have discovered Basia's distress sooner. If only she paid more attention.

Basia throws her book aside. "I don't think undoing the seal the Kler placed on the world is enough. What's the point of any of this if the Kler is still in power? They're the ones deciding how to keep the world running, and the technology is falling to rot. I need them destroyed." She palms her cheeks, wiping up as if to reverse the flow of her tears. "We need to go to Katedra Wieszczów, not try to find the other Strażnicy."

Hanka widens her eyes at Basia. "We do not need to go there for anything."

"I *do*. I need them gone." The witch rises from the table and gestures all around her. "Look, what the Kler has done. The world plunged in darkness for generations. Not having the care to make sure what scant light remains stays lit. They don't even make sure the constructs stay clean, Hanka. I refuse to believe they don't know. They got the power they wanted, and now the rest of the world can fade into ruin."

Basia's breaths come heavy. She spits them out. And her eyes plead with Hanka.

Hanka closes her eyes. She doesn't want to go back to Katedra Wieszczów. Even if it's to destroy it, she doesn't know what the other night-kissed beasts are like now. Her entire brood has matured, and who knows if the Kler let them out into the world or kept them in that cage made of brick and stone. She feels pain whenever her other kin are hurt. She doesn't want to know what the slaughter of her siblings will do to her. If the agony doesn't kill her, the heartbreak might.

"I won't guide you there." She raises a hand before Basia can open her mouth to protest. "I can feel the hurt of the other night-kissed. The Kler will use them as their guards. Also, there's only two of us, and many of them."

"We can fight." Basia balls her hands into fists.

Hanka wants to comfort her, put her hands on hers and sap this excess heat from her. She finds it better to stay further away. "We will die. Unless the technomancers can send others to the Kolebka. Your fellowship can't be the only one."

"We were." Basia falls to the ground, sitting. She covers her face to hide it from Hanka. "They don't know I'm here."

Hanka sighs. It seems she isn't the only one who broke apart from her own. She lowers herself, sitting cross-legged away from Basia. The warmth from the pipes carrying the construct's warmth presses against her bare thighs. She hadn't wanted to put her travel clothes back on. They weren't going anywhere. "What happened, then? How did you get here?"

Basia moves her hands from her cheeks. She breathes so hard, trying to catch her breath as if she just scaled the Wieża steps again. "Our fellowship formed because some of us wanted to see for ourselves if the Kler would uphold their end of the bargain. We got too tired of waiting for the light. The others could wait for however long it would take. We couldn't."

She sniffs loudly before continuing. "Outside of the Kolebka, in the towns where the technomancers lived, thrived, we managed the constructs serving as towns' hearts and engines. We kept them in the square, cleaning them regularly. There are towns out there that aren't ours, towns managed by the Kler. I went to one once. They let me stay with them until one day I asked the Mistrz, if he knows anything from the Kler about the lights coming back now that we'd killed or decommissioned all the constructs. You know what he told me?" Hanka shakes her head. "He told me that they hadn't heard from the Kolebka in some time. When the other technomancers learned of it, most wanted to keep waiting. I couldn't. Neither could some others. So our fellowship left for the Kolebka."

"What happened to them?"

"They perished. Either to the Kler or the beasts, or the journey itself." Basia pauses and doesn't keep going. She flexes her fingers and stares into her palms.

Hanka scoots closer to Basia, close enough that she can feel the warmth radiating from beneath her stockings. Hanka understands the hurt, that isolation. Her anger towards the Kler is more personal, but she got herself out of their influence, and that anger has waned.

"Sorry, I just." Basia sighs. "The Kler put this world in such a state. What's a single good reason why I can't get rid of them?"

Hanka thinks again of her brethren. "Because I'm not going to let you. Eliminating the Kler isn't going to be a good remembrance of your fellowship." She tilts her head thoughtfully, considers another angle. "I don't think you want to be responsible for the world if you do."

Basia swallows. "What do you mean?"

"The Kler took over because they started the Wieczna Noc, right? The world became theirs. And even though they're allowing it to fall to ruin, I don't think you want to helm that collapse either."

"I don't understand."

"What I'm saying is—if we kill the Strażnicy, it's not our responsibility what happens next. That still belongs to the Kler. So, I would much rather guide you to the Strażnicy and undo all the Kler has built. That will destroy them just as well as your sword would. If you'll still protect me, of course."

Basia spreads her hands, palms up. Confused. "You don't even want them dead!"

Hanka thinks of broodmothers and the steep climb to the Katedra's high walls. "Oh, but I *do*. I didn't hesitate in putting down the Strażnik. In death lies freedom too."

Basia presses the heel of her palm into her eye. "Why are you so kind to me? I kill your brethren, both the Kler and the beasts. They're going to hunt you too once they realize what part you played in their demise."

Hanka has been hunted since the moment she escaped. It's nothing new. "I know. But if this darkness is supposedly such a force for good, why does it have so many casualties? Why do so many things need to fall for it to stay in place? Sacrificing the natural order of things should have been more than enough. Instead, the constructs had to die too. If the Kler made more night-kissed constructs, I can't imagine they're in working order either. The Kler has no reverence for the things they created. They don't deserve them." They didn't deserve Hanka. They don't deserve her brethren.

The witch takes heavy breaths, gulping the air like a woman drowning. "You're right. How are you so right?"

Hanka gently takes Basia's wet face in her hands. "Because I see you, Basia. You showed me just how much of a lie everything in this world is. And if helping you free the lights is how I show thanks, then that's what I'll do."

Before Basia can speak again, Hanka presses her mouth to hers. Words aren't needed—they are in this journey together. It would be presumptuous for Hanka to call herself Basia's new fellowship. But this singularity in outcome makes it seem like they could be. They are in this together, brought together by the people keeping this abyss in place.

Basia kisses her back, lips following as if Hanka's are leading a dance. Kissing her offers the kind of comfort that Hanka wishes she hadn't denied herself back in Tawerna. But this is later, and it is better for the wait. They are inside, with all the safety that the architecture confers. Inside, there is light. There is food and drink. There is comfort.

Hanka doesn't have to worry about her or Basia using their hands to enact defense, to preserve themselves with violence. Instead, she reaches beneath the witch's shirt, cool hands gliding over her warm flesh. Her rough thumbs brush against the large swell of her breasts. She helps remove her top, and Hanka sighs at the sight of all her scars and bruises. The story of a life beyond the Droga, from beyond the Kolebka.

A jagged mark crosses from Basia's shoulder across her sternum. Hanka starts kissing her there. Lips press and release the skin with loud smacks. Soft moans, more like grunts, come from Basia's throat, and it's such a sweet sound. Hanka would love to capture it in a tune.

A hand touches Hanka's cheek. "Is this later?"

"It is." Hanka then gathers the hem of her dress and pulls it up and off. Her own skin tells no tale across its features save for several moles and birth marks that cover her pale skin. Light hair the same gold shade as that on her head gathers between her thighs. It's not often that Hanka can smell herself, but the scent of her own wetness is enough to make her clit ache. It's been so long since she touched herself.

And Basia does not hesitate, not even letting Hanka remove her boots or socks. She crawls over, diving straight between her thighs like a bird of prey. Her lips lap and dart against Hanka's folds, strong hands holding her thighs apart. The impatience makes Hanka's heart pound and makes her unafraid to vocalize just how good Basia's mouth feels.

She nearly screams when Basia plunges a pair of fingers into her hole, curling them as they thrust in and out of her. The pace punishes. It's born of desperation, an antidote to despair.

Their sounds echo throughout the archives. She thinks of how her cunt drools against the old carpeting. It's not their mess, not their responsibility. It's evidence that they had been in Stara Baśń. Evidence that they had been here and alive and together.

Hanka arches her back against the floor as she cums, bucking her hips against Basia's face. Relief and care, her body becoming undone. Once the wave passes, she leans up. Basia smirks, her face glistening with Hanka's wetness.

Basia slips her fingers into Hanka's mouth. She laps up her own slick, salty musk fills her nose, and she can't help herself from bobbing against Basia's digits.

"Do you want to taste me next?" Basia asks with a slight chuckle. It suits her so much better than the crying. Hanka nods as best as she can. She wants to etch into her memory the grin Basia gives her. It's tender, it's sharp. It's how Hanka wants to always think of the witch.

Basia pulls away and stands up, removing her boots, then then her socks, then stockings, and the belt holding it up. Her warmer skin glows in the interior lights. Hanka wonders if this is what the Nadziemscy would be like, glowing enough to blind. Her eyes are not worthy of staring at either such beauties.

Basia straddles Hanka's head, pressing her once more down into the rug. Despite how short she is, her pussy seems so far away. But Hanka doesn't have to beg, she simply waits as calmly as she can as muscular thighs swell when Basia lowers herself. Hanka shivers in anticipation. How is she afforded the luxury of such beauty?

The taste is even better than the view. Her cunt is sweet, like warm honey. Hanka's tongue swirls around Basia's puffy lips, making sure she feels each bit of flesh, commits it to memory. It's the one place where Basia is soft, but also where she is hardest. Hanka sucks her clit between her lips, pulling sharp groans as Basia grinds her pelvis against Hanka's face. Breathing becomes a challenge; it's one she's willing to fail.

Her hands reach up and grasp at the meat that is Basia's ass. Taut muscles melt beneath her palms, but resist. It's where Hanka would want to taste next. Her own arousal returns as she thinks of how that flesh would feel in her mouth.

As Basia rides her, Hanka reaches a hand between her legs and flicks at her own clit, chasing the same release Basia had given her earlier. Skin slaps against skin, a ditty of diddling and pleasure. A tune of being together, a song cementing a different kind of fellowship. Something primal and in harmony with itself and its two performers.

Basia hollers as she cums, slick spilling against Hanka's face. She laps at Basia's pussy, not wanting to let even the smallest dribble go to waste. When Basia collects herself, she lifts her hips and falls onto one side. Hanka pulls herself along the rough carpet and nestles her face against Basia's quickly rising chest. Both their hearts pound, off-rhythm with each other, but it's the togetherness that counts.

"I'm not letting you go anywhere alone, I hope you know that," Hanka says, sighing softly against Basia's breast. It's the words that scare her more than learning how she makes Basia feel.

"I know. And I'll be glad to take you with me." Basia kisses the top of her head.

Tiredness and calm cast twin spells on Hanka, enchanting her with sleep's brief oblivion.

IT TAKES SEVERAL MEAL cycles, but eventually they find the maps and directions to the location of the Strażnicy Dwóch Księżyców, the guardians of the twin moons, who reside in an eponymous castle named Zamek Dwóch Księżyców. Such fortresses didn't exist in the slice of the world where Basia had been born. There it was all small towns connected by roads and perhaps a central market district for trade. From what they can tell of the maps, however, Zamek Dwóch Księżyców seems to straddle a few mountains, having its own highway separate from the Droga. At least this time they won't be climbing exterior stairs.

Basia takes the time to sketch the map into her notebook while Hanka looks over, eyes wide with what can only be admiration. "Have you heard of this place, Hanka?" she asks the bard.

"I have not," she replies. "Initiates were not privy to the Nadziemskie Kaplice. I'm not sure if even Patryk knows of their locations."

"Once we kill these Strażnicy, all the Kler will know that someone other than their inner circle knew the locations of all the Strażnicy. How else would two of the three Nadziemscy return otherwise, after having been gone for so long?"

Hanka nods and grunts softly. "We shouldn't be striking the Kler first, but if they're going to attack us, it'd be good to prepare for that encounter."

Basia looks over at Hanka. Her finger has healed—or rather, there is a digit that matches the one on her left hand. "It seems you're done healing."

Surprised, Hanka lifts her palm. "You're right. I was wondering how long that would be missing."

"I'm glad the answer is, 'Not long at all.' I know I wouldn't be able to regenerate like that." It's the softest lie. The resurrection stone probably can, but that bit of technomancy should only be reserved for death, not dismemberment. Basia wouldn't dare be so wasteful.

Though, as they're setting out for the next battle, Basia decides it's time to tell Hanka about the tool.

"There's something I want to show you," she says. She sets her notebook aside and lets the ink dry.

Beside her, the backpack sits with its flap open. Its strong leather and fabric sides have grooves from the clothes, the notebooks, the provisions, and the spent resurrection stones piled within it. She reaches inside, pushing past her other things to reach where the stones sit on the bottom. The long hexagonal stones are dark with their sharp points broken off where they had pierced the deceased. Only one remains active, shimmering faintly with a pale yellow glow that Basia heard had been described as dawn's light. When the point pierces a technomancer's flesh, the stone floods the technomancer with sun-embraced magic, pulling the very fibers of their being back into working order. They don't all come back exactly the same, much in the same way that sleep can leave one refreshed or ruined. She's prepared herself for transformation.

But it's not one she can administer onto herself.

Hanka straightens, leaning over to see into the backpack's mouth. "What is that?"

Basia pulls out the stone. It weighs heavily in her hand, like it knows it's not an object to be used frivolously. "All the technomancers who entered the Kolebka had one of these. These resurrection stones made it so that we had twenty-six of us, rather than thirteen. It can be used to bring a person back to life exactly one time. I carry the twelve already spent stones with me; this last one is mine."

"Does it come with instructions?"

"It does." Basia takes the stone and points its sharp end to just below her sternum. "If I die, you take the stone and plunge it into my stomach. It will break, so there's only the one time you can use it. And it doesn't matter what state my body is in, but you must strike somewhere around my stomach."

"You say this from personal experience?"

Basia had tried using it on Marisia's arm. The resurrection spell was wasted in that futile attempt. "Unfortunately."

"You've carried the other twelve with you." It's not a question.

"Yes."

Hanka scoots her chair closer and places a hand under Basia's chin, tilting her head up. "I'm so sorry. No wonder you've hated being alone. I'll use the stone when it's time, I promise."

Basia lets the stone fall into her backpack, clinking against its spent brethren. It doesn't break. The other cracked stones have not even left a scratch on its shiny surface. One day, she'll have to clear the dust that's settled at the bottom of her pack, but it won't be soon. "When the time comes, just strike as hard as you can."

"I can do that." Hanka smiles widely at her, though it doesn't quite reach her eyes. Why would it? Hanka has only just promised to bring Basia back to life should the situation call for it.

All Basia can offer is a tight-lipped purse almost like a smirk in return. She returns to her notes. "Have you found anything about the last Strażnik?"

Hanka returns to her own work area and stares at the papers strewn about and the books laid flat open. There's a lot that Basia recognizes could be about the same thing, but she's not sure. The Kler created their own damn script to keep anyone else out.

"It's only things I knew about already, like the stories of how the sun was exiled atop Ołtarz Słońca." Before Basia gets mad, she adds, "Only saying that was where it happened, not where it is or what it looks like."

"Do you think it'd be near the Katedra?"

"I'm *not* taking you to the Katedra."

Basia looks at the map Hanka had drawn for her. The Katedra is clearly marked—it's much closer to Stara Baśń than Basia ever expected. She looks at Hanka then back at the page. "You trust me enough to tell me where it is?"

"You've been true to your promise of protecting me. And you can't protect me if you go there."

"Do you not think I can take them?"

"Not on your own and not with me at your side." Hanka crosses her arms. "I've already told you: I'm not going to attack my own kin if I can avoid it."

"I heard you the first time." Basia massages her temples. She knows that even if information about the Ołtarz can be found in the Katedra, Hanka will not take her to it. It's why the bard frankly searches for anything else while Basia collects herself from her annoyance. The silence is another presence in this room, filling the space with its nothingness. It's almost like the darkness, but that stays securely beyond these walls and their lanterns powered by the construct below.

The next meal has passed before Hanka mutters, "I think I found something. It's not much, but it's something."

Basia gnaws on the inside of her cheek, keeping her patience in check. Between the two of them, they possess only the barest of literacy in terms of the Kler's texts. She needs to be calm, and she cannot rush Hanka, as much as she needs to know. Distraction is their enemy. As much as she personally wants to exact violent vengeance, a small part of Basia remains that knows better. The Kler cannot be defeated directly—they need to lose their power otherwise.

It's what gave Stara Baśń its opportunity for sovereignty. It can happen across the Kolebka too.

"Something?" she prompts.

"It's a plateau towards the north. It used to be called Szczyt Świata, but now it's the Ołtarz." Hanka leans in, looks over the passage once again. "It used to *be* Szczyt Świata, but the Kler flattened it, then placed the sun there."

"Bastards." Everything they've ever touched is now a ruin. "How's the climb?"

"Stairs. Many stairs. A spiral." Hanka drags her finger against the page in loops. "I think we can make it though, assuming the Kler aren't also after us."

"And how would they be able to do such climbs?" Basia doesn't imagine they got much conditioning done, not with how much time they spend researching crimes against the living.

"The Katedra has many stairs. It's a place built for giants, not for short people like us. I remember running from building to building, alcove to alcove. There were many departments and halls, all stacked upon each other. Stara Baśń and Tawerna were both easy to learn in comparison, it's why I could get us out of Tawerna as quickly as we did."

"So, how did the Kler know to find us?"

"The same way I recognized you—all magic leaves a mark. I hadn't cast in a while, which made it really easy to hide in Tawerna. You, on the other hand, I easily saw your glow. It reminded me of someone I knew in the Katedra."

Basia stares at Hanka. A glow like Basia's only meant one thing. "There was a technomancer in the Katedra?"

Hanka nods. "There was one, yes. I don't think they made it out when I left. They're the one who gifted me the balalaika."

"That explains why someone who can cast the darkness can cast with the sun's embrace—it's all the same magic, isn't it?"

Hanka shrugs. "There's no way for any of us to know. The Kler might. But I think what would make for a better world is if we didn't keep the light and the dark so separate from each other. There's got to be something better than a world overrun with constructs or a world completely smothered."

Basia clicks her teeth. "I don't think that's our responsibility."

"It isn't. Which is why we're going to free the lights and then leave the world to the Kler and whoever remains to run it. I think Stara Baśń will fare well in the Mistrz's hands. I can't say the same for the other towns and cities."

"Maybe the Katedra will fall on its own." It's a thought that brings Basia comfort. She still desires to personally ram her blade through them and set the Kler ablaze, but if a crisis of faith means the priests turn on each other, then she'll be patient and allow it.

Hanka hesitates before saying, "Would you like to know that my escape almost guaranteed it?"

The question surprises Basia. "Really? How much damage could a bard have done?"

Hanka lets out a sigh that could've been a laugh, but Basia doesn't think further than that. "I didn't like how they kept the technomancer. Much like the construct, the Kler kept them in a cell. So, I offered to let them go. Maybe they could have met up with your fellowship, or maybe they could have left the Kolebka altogether. They had stayed because they wanted to aid the Kler in creating other constructs, but it wasn't working because they refused to use the sun's embrace."

"Of course." Basia rolls her eyes. It's the stubbornness that pisses her off the most. It's the absolute refusal to make anything better for the people still trapped in this abyss.

"They wanted the world to be dependent on them." Hanka stalls by drinking some more water. "Since I wanted to leave anyway because I didn't want to become a broodmother, I offered to take the technomancer with me. That was a mistake. Their presence alerted all the beasts in the Katedra. They didn't make it out."

Basia shivers. Of course, the Kler wouldn't let a technomancer survive in these lands without being tethered to them. She doesn't know who that technomancer could have been. The most likely assumption is that they were born in the Kolebka after the exile. Or that there are other technomancers, and their shit luck got them into the hands of the Kler. Basia has never believed that the priests could have cast out all the technomancers. The Kolebka is simply too large, with too many people living in it. Some would have survived the purge.

"I'm sorry for your loss," Basia says. "It's not your fault, you know that, right?"

Hanka won't look at her. "I still feel like I led them into a trap. One that only I survived."

Basia knows Hanka isn't the only one who survived—there was the man who recognized her in Tawerna. "What about the priest you know? Pa-something."

"Patryk." There's no contempt in the way Hanka corrects her. "We saw him. He didn't follow me when I first escaped. To be honest, I'm grateful."

There's no reason for Basia to be polite. They're going to destroy the world, so she might as well be blunt with Hanka. "We're probably going to have to kill him if he gets in our way."

Hanka's lips quiver. "I think you're right. I hope, for both our sakes, he doesn't follow us. He might not even know about the Ołtarz. Why would a beast need to know?"

"Did you put that information in the notebook yet?"

The notebook is open to page full of notes and drawings. Hanka flaps her hand, blowing the archives' stale wind across the ink to help it dry. "It is now!" The bard holds up the crinkling pages and drags her fingers from the crude illustration of lofted Stara Baśń to Katedra Wieszczów marked with triangles and arcs that Basia thinks are supposed to represent towers and buttresses, to a plate with something that could resemble a star on it. The depictions are rudimentary. In fact, they're enough to make Basia giggle. They're minimally useful.

"What are you laughing at?"

"It's so different than how I would've drawn it. But there's no point in correcting." She stands from her seat. "If we know where we're going, we should leave. We've been guests here for far longer than I would have cared for."

Hanka nods in agreement and starts putting away the tomes they had taken out while Basia puts away the writing implements and the precious directions. It seems strange that she once worried she would have to eliminate the Strażnicy on her own. With Hanka, her cleverness, and her beast's ability to see in the dark, Basia feels even more that it might be possible. Perhaps she told Hanka of the resurrection stone for nothing. Maybe it won't be used after all; it can just be a remnant of this age of darkness for them to carry into a future of light.

One of the Mistrz's staff greets them as they leave the archives. There must have been some cleaning done since the people of Stara Baśń eliminated the Kler—in contrast to how mussed everyone looked when they first arrived, this servant wears an unstained and unwrinkled gray uniform of straight trousers and a jacket with two parallel sets of buttons along the front. A blue triangular scarf sits tucked into their neckline.

"Leaving already? Do you want me to report anything to the Mistrz?" they ask.

"Yes," Basia says. "Tell the Mistrz that we're going to get out of his hair."

The servant nods and goes to find the Mistrz while Basia and Hanka return to their room.

They prepare in silence. Despite having seen each other naked and enjoyed the way they played with each other's flesh, they get dressed with their backs turned. As much as Basia would love to stare at Hanka's unclothed form, she needs to stay focused on the defensive way she layers her clothes. The tight single piece that traps most of her warmth, the armored chest piece with the pocket for her resurrection stone, the trousers, the belt of knives. She had set off to the Kolebka with movement and defense in mind. She wants to concentrate on getting dressed in exactly the same way. It's served her so far.

It will also make it easier to protect Hanka from the Strażnicy waiting for them in the Kler's Nadziemskie Kaplice.

As they head down to the entryway, dozens more staff members greet them with small, lumpy burlap sacks filled with provisions. Basia isn't sure if the two of them will need that much food, but Hanka takes and packs them carefully into her bag. She's the one with the spare space, because she's not weighing herself down with relics of her fallen companions.

Once the sun returns, Basia will figure out where best to bury the spent resurrection stones. It's the least she can do to honor their memories.

The Mistrz's Estate's doors open revealing that a throng has come out into the Estate's square to see the two of them off. Basia has never been in a place where hundreds, if not more, can gather, all carrying their own lanterns despite the lights returned to Stara Baśń. The warm glow soothes the tiredness from the laypeople's exhausted faces. Something else glimmers in their eyes—hope. The Kler took that from them. Basia doesn't think it's something that she and Hanka will be returning to them, but if it's one of the consequences of bringing the Nadziemscy back, then she will accept that responsibility.

As the two of them walk down towards the streets, the crowds part for them. Silence overtakes the square, but unlike the soundless wastes of the Kolebka, there's something comforting in this lack of noise. Calm permeates through these people, radiating towards Hanka and Basia.

When they reach Stara Baśń's exit, the Baśni Mistrz stands and awaits them. He wears a plush coat in a thick, shining fabric Basia had never seen before. Loose, sable trousers almost like a skirt hug his legs—borrowed attire from the Kler. He leans on his staff and grins at the pair. "Do you two have everything you need?"

Hanka gives Basia a small nod.

"I'm not sure what other provisions we need, panie," Basia says. As if talking about it reminds her of its weight, Basia feels the bag weighing heavily on her back, robust with the food and her flasks and remembrances of the fallen.

"You have our hope and our blessing," he replies.

"And do you have what you need?" Hanka asks, forgetting the honorific.

He grins at them. "The Kler is gone. The lights are back on. I think we have what we need until those priests show up at these doors again."

"Make sure to keep an eye on that sluice," Hanka reminds him.

"I've already stationed guards there. You don't need to worry about us."

Basia will never consider them ever again. The exchange of resources and information was helpful and learning about the city construct's decay and the corruption of night-kissed beasts into new constructs once again set her heart aflame against the Kler, but those things could have happened without Stara Baśń.

However, it also gave her an annoyance that simmers because of Hanka not letting her enact any kind of vengeance. Freeing the Nadziemscy from the Strażnicy isn't enough; Basia needs the Kolebka stained with the Kler's blood. It's a rage and a desire for violence almost as fierce as the tenderness Basia feels for Hanka. It's Hanka that's keeping her together, even if Basia wishes the tether weren't there. But that's the fault of having to travel with a companion, this duet of a fellowship. She cannot act of her own volition, even though her selfishness has ensured her survival this far.

"This is farewell, Baśńi Mistrz," Basia says. She turns on one foot.

From the corner of her eye, she sees him bow. "Next time we see each other, the sun will have risen many times over."

The crowd roars with cheers and calls rumbling like a storm. They wish Hanka and Basia haste and luck on their mission. The way the people of Stara Baśń bid them farewell feels more deserving for heroes of a great tale, not two lonely and pissed off bitches looking to cause problems for the priests that wronged them. The hand that was meant to care for this world has its rescinded kindness. Such neglect deserves consequences.

The enormous gates to Stara Baśń open. Frost falls from the decorative steel flowers as the doors scrape against the ground, revealing the way back onto the Droga and out into the Kolebka, whose sky now glitters with stars like powdered snow.

CHAPTER NINE

THE CASTLE OF THE TWIN MOONS

DAREK: HE TOLD ME HE LIVED IN HIS OWN MANSION

HANKA FINDS THE ZAMEK Dwóch Księżyców not by the sight of night's kiss on its facade (there is none), not by the single strip of the Droga that trails down the middle of the long highway up to the castle, but by the singing whose familiarity chills her down to her marrow. It's soft, and it begs. Children calling out to a parent. Children begging for food. Children begging for attention.

She once sang a similar song.

Basia continues onward, but Hanka stops. Her feet stay rooted to the mouth of the bridge that connects to the Zamek's main entrance. She sees it, looming and gray in the endless night. What this place had been used for before the Zaćmienie is anyone's guess. But now, it sounds exactly like a nursery, its hymn the exact same piece that keeps her away from the Katedra, that wants her to keep *Basia* away from the Katedra.

"What's wrong?" the witch asks. The lit charm on her swords bathes the two of them in light.

"Can't you hear it?" Hanka replies, voice soft. "You can't hear the singing?"

Basia cranes her neck back, closing her eyes. She breathes slowly. It would be silent if not for the fact that Hanka can almost count how many voices are coming from the Zamek. There are hundreds. And she thought the only nursery for night-kissed beasts was in the Katedra.

"I don't hear anything." It doesn't sound like denial or an accusation, just an unfortunate truth. There's no reason for the technomancer to have any connection to the brood of night's kiss.

Pressure builds in Hanka's eyes. It's been a while since she last cried, but this isn't grief, this is fear. "I don't know what I expected, but I didn't expect to hear my kin."

The witch puts her hands on Hanka's upper arms in comfort. Hanka likes it when Basia touches her. It soothes the cold running through her flesh, but there's nothing the witch can do or say to provide solace. The edge of her blade is going to cut through Hanka's kin, and there's nothing the bard can do about it without putting both herself and Basia in harm's way.

Hanka leans into that warmth. "You can try to spare them, can't you?"

"Trying is all I've got," Basia replies. "As long as they don't attack us. I cannot guarantee their safety if they do."

Hanka takes a shuddering breath. The words struggle to meet her throat. It's going to hurt a lot. Whatever encounter they have, it's going to end in pain. She briefly considers letting Basia go forth on her own, but she can't see anything. The only light she has is her own, not beast's eyes that can peer through the darkness.

The witch's hand falls, clasping delicately around Hanka's. "I can't do this without you."

"I know." Then stronger, she repeats, "I know. I'm sorry. I'm usually not afraid of pain, but—"

"I'll save my blade for the Strażnik." Basia turns, taking Hanka's hand and gently pulling her across the bridge.

They walk at the border of the Droga's light. They don't want to be in its glow; unwanted eyes will find them there, signal a warning. If the night-kissed inside the Zamek don't see them coming, Hanka will feel better.

It's a long crossing over the bridge, her kin's song growing louder and louder the closer they get. Surely, Basia must hear it. But Hanka looks over at her companion, and the witch's expression hasn't changed.

"You still can't hear them, can you?" Hanka asks.

"I cannot, no. I believe you when you say you can. Are they loud?"

"They're loud, but it's not painful." In fact, the song comforts with its familiarity, even though she left the nursery where she had been born. She doesn't know what became of the beasts of her brood, if they're still even alive. They might be wandering the Kolebka as they speak, hunting for people who have wandered off the Droga and into its wilderness. At least they can quickly hide in those protective lights should trouble come. Most night-kissed beasts can't cross onto it—that Hanka and Patryk could was another sign of their humanity. But she isn't sure if Basia can—she cannot imagine the Kler making it easy for a technomancer to get into the Kolebka at all, let alone wander the partitioned, winding river that is its surface.

Much like the road to both Stara Baśń and the Wieża, the Droga ends at the foot of the Zamek's large stairs. Both Basia and Hanka have to lift their legs high, like dancers, to get to the next step. It's not meant for people. It's likely for the larger beasts, the ones who might trip from steps too short or too narrow. She and Patryk had always been smaller, both as beasts and beasts in a human form. The result is a hard climb, but not as difficult as the Wieża's stairs.

At the top they find two enormous, brass doors facing them. Etched into their surface are twin depictions of moons casting their light upon small groups of people gathered around a great lake with sweeping waves that look like they're dancing. The Zamek must have been built before the Zaćmienie. No one has seen the moons in so long, and the Kler only makes art that celebrates the darkness.

It's as if they had wanted people to forget, with time, that there ever were lights.

If that is what they wanted, they should have done more to prevent their artificial replacements for the Nadziemscy from falling apart.

"Hanka," Basia calls from the left. "I found a way in."

It's a much smaller door adjacent to the metal slabs. There was no moving those, and Hanka guesses that Basia has been around enough buildings and settlements to know of side entrances, much like Hanka had quickly learned Tawerna's ins and outs.

The witch doesn't try to push the door open. She ignites her sword, raises it over her head, and rails on the wooden exterior. It splinters and breaks beneath the heat warping it and the metal crashing into it. Hanka winces with each strike. Each one shrieks, sending unpleasantness up her arm that has her shivering. It's also the crescendo of her kin's songs—they know danger is coming. They know something enters that shouldn't be allowed within these titanic walls.

Basia exhales as the hinges creak open, the door's charred remains sprinkling ash onto the ground. "Let's go."

The song breaks. A cacophony of screams infiltrate Hanka's mind. The beasts know the two of them are coming. Hanka pauses in the doorway, so Basia takes her hand again and drags her through the tight side entrance. The walls have never felt closer—the light from Basia's sword only shows off the dust gathered in the corner and blemishes from years of misuse.

Unlike in Tawerna, where the side door led to a pantry and more open spaces, this one simply guides them a narrow flight of stairs. The song returns to its harmony as quickly as it had ruptured into a panic and Hanka wonders what defenses this nursery has in place, what protections the brood seeks for itself. Do they not fear Basia? Hanka remembers when she had been young. Her brood would curl together into a mass, gathering their night-kissed magic and prepared to attack. It's how Hanka remembered how to summon the spear she used against the Strażnik despite not using the ability for so long. She wonders if she should warn Basia.

She hopes the Kler wouldn't be so cruel to keep a nursery in the same place they sequestered a Strażnik.

Unless, the nurseries are the Strażnicy's guards, and the beast Basia had killed outside of Gwiedzna Wieża simply didn't create life. Not all night-kissed beasts beget other night-kissed beasts, much how all humans don't always birth other humans. Nature can be cruelly unreliable in that way.

Hanka shakes her head as she climbs the narrow inner stairs. Even with that uncertainty, everything else the Kler has touched with their magic since that first rebellion had been in the name of developing tools. Creating night-kissed beasts to protect the Strażnicy should not be beyond possibility.

And yet it feels as if it should be.

The animals raised for meat and eggs throughout the Kolebka are treated with something like respect. They're given care. Some of the creatures are even named before their violent ends. The Kler, meanwhile, simply sequester their beasts to their nurseries before using them. The cruelty almost calls to question the breadth of Hanka's own imagination.

She regrets that her own fear and haste in her escape from the Katedra led to so much death, that her bravery now may lead to more. It's not fair to the beasts. The Kler is the cause behind her escape and her isolation, the cruelty toward her kin. They are the reason the world is so partitioned. They're the cause of the silence.

As much as Hanka doesn't want to harm her kin, their calls only get louder and louder the higher they climb. The interior of the Zamek feels like the stairs that led up to the Wieża, but indoors. Here there is none of the Kolebka's ceaseless frost, but absent too is the cool mountain air that had wicked her sweat away. Here, the damp gathers at her neck, making her scarf feel heavier than it needs to be. It collects in her elbows and along the back of her knees. The air itself smells warm like kindling.

She looks back to Basia. Though her face gleams with the dew reflecting the scant light from her sword, the witch doesn't seem to be suffering. In fact, there is a clarity in her dark brown eyes. Perhaps it's the strenuousness of this climb or Basia's light itself that makes Hanka's skin warm. It cannot just be the way her night-kissed body rebels against bringing harm to her night-kissed kin.

Where the song is loudest, on the fifth landing, there is a door. Hanka looks at it carefully, examining the latch that keeps the wood in place. It bites at her fingers when she touches it.

Without saying a word, Basia reaches forward. Her hands aglow with magic, a protection against whatever enchantment the Kler could have possibly put on it. The door opens easily beneath her touch. It opens silently and Hanka braces herself to meet a crowd of night-kissed beasts as tightly packed as the throng of humans that bid Hanka and Basia such a fond farewell when they left Stara Baśń.

Instead, the door opens to a hallway which separates them from another large set of double doors. These, however, are just barely taller than Hanka or Basia—a height designed for people to traverse, not intended for whatever behemoth the Zamek's entryway had been designed for.

Hanka's stomach sinks. Her kin start screaming again. She tries not to frighten Basia, not clue the witch into her distress. She steadies her shuddering breaths.

As Basia places both hands on one of the doors, they open, revealing an audience chamber transformed into a night-kissed nursery.

BASIA STEPS INTO THE room, and she understands what Hanka might have been hearing during the entirety of their approach to the Zamek. A swarm of night-kissed beasts skitter against the checkered marble floor. These beasts are nowhere near as large as the carcinoid knight that had defended the entrance into the Gwiedzna Wieża, but they aren't small either. They don't gather close to the door, so she can't accurately guess their size. If Basia had to guess, they come up to her knees. Tattered cloaks of flayed flesh and carapace like shredded attire hang off their bodies. It slaps against the ground as their pointed feet patter against the filthy floor.

She drops her backpack and unsheathes her sword. Hanka puts her hand on Basia's shoulder and points forward.

At the far center of the space sits a mound of these things climbing on top of each other like insects upon refuse. Basia narrows her gaze, trying to pry apart features from competing shadows created by her sword and the mysterious bright, pale light bathing this lofted chamber with its broken and abandoned pews, its ragged tapestries whose designs have long faded to the wounds of abandonment. From where the torn fabric beneath the central pile reveals arms and legs, Basia recognizes scaffolding. Some of these creatures cannot move along the surface. What looks like movement is the futility of stuck arms and glued legs. Whatever the process is by which they grow flesh and carapaces, the tender shells grow atop one another. It seems a slow, painful process.

The structure shifts as if it notices Hanka and Basia's presence in the room. A metallic scent pricks Basia's nose and the thick smell of oil runs down the back of her throat. Both ignite her anger once again.

The Kler has been using nascent night-kissed beasts to craft another construct.

The constructs of the technomancers came to life with magic, not having technology and metallurgy forcefully grafted onto life itself. It does not make it better that not all of the creatures are merged together. The ones that manage to bop along the ground have metal plates protruding from their fleshy heads, pressed tightly like skullcaps onto bone and skin. With each movement, black liquid that is neither blood nor oil drips down their arms. Chains wrap around gears which make their limbs move as their busy hands work hastily to arrange new shapes and forms hidden and stuck to the mass.

These creatures are mixtures of mechanics and magic to form a new tool that shouldn't exist.

"They've stopped singing," Hanka says, softly. Her vertical pupils are thin lines. She trembles.

All movement in the room stops. Perhaps Hanka and Basia's presence deactivated them. somehow. With the shallow way Hanka breathes, Basia doubts it.

With nothing moving, Basia sees the intention of this amalgamation of flesh, metal, and magic. She's seen the insides and the process for decommissioning a construct, the process by which the organs within it that respond to the sun's embrace are removed and replaced with machinery. This is the opposite, in every way. The creatures that are too large to fit inside force the smaller ones into the crevasses. Others that have spindly, two-fingered hands pull their fellows apart. Some hold onto each other for a reason unknown to her. Only technomancers should be in the sorcery of crafting constructs. It should not be left to tiny living things without even a priest to guide the process.

Basia's grip around her sword's hilt tightens. She wants to cast the spell to ignite her sword, and not just her sword, every item and piece of machinery in this room. The Kler wants to prolong this night, make the uninhabitable world ceaseless. She can't let that happen. The surest way to start healing the world from its isolation and degradation is to free the Nadziemscy.

The creatures start moving again in a retreat. They climb off the scaffold upon which they cling and crawl on top of each other. Some fall off from the tallest supports. Fleshy bodies hit the stone floor with a smack, followed by a crunch. Hanka winces with each impact. Basia's hopes sink—this is a battle she'll need to fight on her own. The bard will feel every injury, and even if she can defeat these beasts, then Basia will need to protect her while also fighting through a pair of Strażnicy.

If only she had the rest of her fellowship.

"Hanka, what are they doing?" Basia cannot keep the anger from her voice. The Kler clearly got impatient waiting for another pair like Hanka and Patryk to be born. They didn't have the patience for the research required to make true constructs, so they're trying to turn living things into new machinery.

The bard swallows hard as she takes her balalaika and prepares it for a performance. "They're dressing the Strażnicy."

Basia snaps her head to look at the bard. "Strażnicy?"

"There's two of them. One for each moon."

The beasts' joints and jaws chitter while their feet and hands clatter. They crawl all over each other, moving like a swarm. The ones made of more congealed bodies are pried apart by their mobile brethren. It's a chorus of scraping and sloshing.

"Are they saying anything?" The words come out more panicked than Basia intended.

"They're singing about the moons."

Instead of gathering towards Hanka and Basia, the beast-constructs form an organized line along the sides of this throne room, encircling the base of the columns holding the vaulted ceiling up. They climb over each other, rising higher and higher, a new structure of meat and metal.

The smell makes Basia want to wretch. It's burnt oil, it's seared flesh, it's festering wounds. Death would be a kindness; they wouldn't even have to beg her for it.

The night-kissed that remain along the scaffold do not move. The little beasts hang onto the poorly-built bent arms of the beast-construct. Its elbows bow under the weight, curving at a strenuous angle. Its head is a blank slate marred from where bodies fell off—the scars make something like a face, but it's clear the Kler had no design intent. Along the construct's torso remains a large panel of the more nascent night-kissed. Tiny hands grip tightly, holding the seams closed. With a gust of wind like an exhale, the creatures let go of each other's hands at the same time. The audience chamber's pale light intensifies. Basia raises a hand to shield her eyes.

From within the cavern that opens in the construct's chest emerge different constructs that are more frighteningly familiar to Basia. They are dolls not unlike the Strażnik Astralny: small enough to fit within the unfinished night-kissed construct, but still towering over the smaller beasts.

Much like the fabric into which the stars were threaded, the Strażnicy Dwóch Księżyców hold the moons like helms in place of their heads. Twin blue orbs cast new lights and new shadows. Cloaks of brilliant white cascade from their pointed shoulders like curtains against their narrow, metallic frames. They stand on avian legs bent backward with rusty mist coming from their joints—these constructs have not seen movement in quite some time. While they hold hands, the opposite arms carry great, curved swords gleaming in their mimicry of the moons' light. The blue steel shines like fire. There are no mouths with which for them to speak.

As if reading Basia's mind, Hanka says, "They're not saying anything. I can't hear the constructs."

"And what of the night-kissed?"

"Chanting. I can't make out the words, though."

Basia immediately starts forming a strategy in her mind. The Strażnicy Dwóch Księżyców will leap, and leap far. They will blind her with the brightness of their visages. The swords, she has no plan for, aside from avoiding injury and dismemberment.

The thing she knows she can't do is rely on Hanka. It hurts her heart to think of the bard that way, but if errant wounds on the nearby beasts from the skirmish between the Strażnicy and Basia is going to bring harm to Hanka, she'd rather do this fight on her own.

Angry tears gather in the corners of her eyes. If only her fellowship hadn't fallen. If only she had more than a single resurrection stone to rely on. If only they hadn't all died so quickly after arriving in the Kolebka. If she had anyone else without a connection to the things holding the Nadziemscy back.

The Strażnicy Dwóch Księżyców bend their arms, swinging their swords in front of them such that their tips kiss twice with a metal clang.

Basia shouts, "Rozpalić!" Flames engulf her sword. The bright trail follows after her as she dashes her way across into the center of the audience chamber. Her boots hit the stone hard, soles slapping against the ground. She leaves Hanka behind; if the bard stays away from this fight, she won't get hurt through the peripheral injuries of her kin.

It is a perfect plan to have Basia do the fighting alone. As much as she values Hanka as a companion, she cannot rely on the bard as a fighter. She's simply a guide, after all, and it's Basia's job to protect her.

With their swords aloft and alight, the Strażnicy Dwóch Księżyców lumber towards Basia. Their heavy bodies leave loud, resounding steps. They angle their swords carefully such that the tips do not scrape against the ground and prepare to strike. They move like a couple committing to each other in rituals Basia has only ever read about. Basia crouches and launches herself into the air. Following the swing of her sword, she spins in mid-air. Her flames arch behind her like a tail as she slashes towards the Strażnicy. Fiery tongues lick at the air, kissing the Strażnicy's blades. The impact of Basia's sword against theirs hits her with enough force to send her careening across the smooth floor. Despite the Strażnicy's slim, narrow frames, they hit harder than anything Basia has fought yet.

A ringing in her ears replaces the roar of fire as it sweeps over the dust littering the ground's surface. Of her fellowship, Basia had been the most reckless, but the least averse to risks like attacking head on. Elimination before anything else.

She picks herself up, shouting the spell again, the sun-embraced fire growing brighter and whiter. Her sword grows to twice its length in lashing flames. With a holler, she dashes towards the Strażnicy again. One foot put in front of the other, she grips her sword tightly and spins. It's an elegant maneuver that gets swiftly beneath the Strażnicy's heavy swings. Her sword's heat catches the constructs' legs, followed by the metal striking the limbs like the hammer of a bell.

They do not fall.

One twists its head towards Basia, while the other looks towards Hanka. Basia moves before she thinks. She collects her footing and once again dances towards them. Her sword clashes against the steel of the right Strażnik, the one looking towards Hanka. It makes her stumble, but she doesn't relent. She needs to be as annoying as insect, keeping them away from Hanka for as long as it takes Basia to uncover their failure point. Every construct has one, usually in the torso. But there are two torsos. Would she have to destroy one then the other? What if they must be destroyed at the same time because having one body intact means the other never dies?

There were members of her fellowship who could much quicker identify weaknesses than Basia can, but they also didn't have the proficiency with offensive spellcraft that she does. It's that noncommittal expertise that's protected her in the Kolebka thus far. Basia will figure it out; she must. She's the technomancer, and the one who wants to free the moons most.

Basia hears Hanka plucking at her balalaika. Above Basia's head, shards of sun-embraced light shoot through the air like arrows. They hiss as they twinkle, screeching as they shatter against the Strażnicy's metal chassis. Each impact leaves a little crater in the Strażnicy's armor. It's enough to make them stagger. A hard swing of Basia's sword might make it possible to knock them down.

Yelling, she attacks again. Before her sword can land, the Strażnicy cast a spell. A sphere bright and white as the snow smothering the banks of the Droga bursts like a pulse. Cold as wet iron during a blizzard, the spell stings Basia's skin, forcing her to shut her eyes. It freezes her in place. Her sword's flame weakens.

She cannot shake the frost. Uninterrupted by either sun-embraced shards or Basia's attacks, the Strażnicy glide towards Hanka. The sun's embrace in the form of the moon's frigid light dissolves every shard that comes towards the Strażnicy. Hanka switches her tune, the shards of light from her balalaika becoming an even darker black as they grow hotter and hotter. Instead of a graceful launch, they fall heavily at the Strażnicy's feet as they approach. The newly formed hollows in the shattered marble should make them stumble. They are not deterred.

Basia trembles, but to no avail. The cold traps her. There's no way for her to get to Hanka. She will fail once again, but none of the anger roiling within her is enough to coax her body back into action.

Hanka stands her ground. If she moves closer to the entrance, she will compromise their provisions. As the Strażnicy approach, she stops her song. She lifts the balalaika in front of her, as if the delicate wood is any substitute for a shield. The Strażnicy break it into splinters with only a few alternating swings.

Hanka has no way of defending herself, Basia realizes, her heart heavy with fear and doubt. Even with the magic gathered from consuming her own finger, Hanka does not stand a chance, and Basia cannot get her chilled flesh to move.

The Strażnicy flank Hanka from opposite sides, encircling her with their fingers entwined. Unless the bard can duck beneath them and use that tenacity to run away, there's no way out. She wants to scream, but these constructs have Basia paralyzed with magic and Hanka trapped.

They pull back their sword arms and plunge their blades into Hanka. One through her chest by her left shoulder. One through her lower stomach on the right.

If she makes any sounds of pain or agony, Basia cannot hear them. The only sounds running through her head are the roars of her own fury. Hanka wasn't supposed to be fighting, but her spells cast cracks into those smooth faces. Basia wouldn't have stood a chance without her. It's up to her to protect herself, to take down the last things standing between the world and a brightly lit night.

"Rozpalić, rozpalić, *rozpal ich wszyscy,*" she hollers, the words expelling from her lips like violent retching.

A conflagration bursts from her sword, spewing like a geyser, splashing flames throughout the audience chamber. Some of it catches on Basia's clothes, and if it destroys her armor, so be it. She can get on without it. They took Hanka from her, and where this rage is going, she won't need clothes or armor. It will destroy her and the Strażnicy.

Even if one of them survives this, Hanka will still be gone.

The rest of the pyre catches on the clothes and flesh of the spectating night-kissed beasts. She cannot hear whatever sounds they might be making over the roar of her magic and the way her heart thunders in her ears. They might be shrieking, high-pitched tones rising and bursting above the other din.

She doesn't care about the night-kissed beasts; Hanka cannot hear them anymore.

Basia lifts her sword and swings it over her head round and round. Fire leaps from the blade, settling upon the bodies of the beasts. The fire catches against the unfinished night-kissed construct. The Strażnicy panic in a dance that makes them swirl around each other. There's nowhere for them to go—fire swallows their womb. They won't make it to the exit with the conflagrated trap Basia has sprung.

Using her anger to propel herself, Basia jumps into the air. The heat interrupts the Strażnicy's vision, making it easy for the witch to land on one of them. The flames will not end it, but brute force will. She plunges her lit sword deep into the Strażnik's chest, stunning it as the blade sinks deep inside. The chassis trembles, trying to knock Basia off. She holds on tightly, angling her body and her blade such that it twists, cutting through machinery and engineering.

Once the construct stops moving, she twists around and yanks the blade from its target as she leaps off. Black blood spews like a broken damn; she recognizes it as a corruption of the fluid flowing through most technomancer constructs. There will be no pity for this aberration.

As one half falls, the other pushes forward, pulling at its sibling, trying to undo the damage and disorientation committed against its form. Instead, the wounded Strażnik falls. Its glass head smashes into the ground. Shards shatter and spew in a neat, glittering cone. Moonlight beams from the injury like exposed muscle. The light burns through the night-kissed in its path, reducing the burning bodies to dust.

Its attached and frightened sibling teeters forward, bending under the weight of the other Strażnik's fall. Basia pants. Her muscles scream for relief, for purchase, while the smell of char and ash fills her nose. It makes her mouth water in that way it always does before her stomach's contents wind up on the wrong side of her body. She fights to ignore it; she can't be distracted by her own biological distress.

The remaining Strażnik takes its sword and smashes it against hands entwined. It takes one, two, three hits to wreck the places where the fingers connected into conjoined hands. They do not come apart neatly. Digits break off and fall against the ground. The Strażnik rips apart its joints to free itself from its deceased twin's grasp.

Basia doesn't give it a chance. With the same ferocity, she lifts herself with magic and stabs the other Strażnik. It falls backward, carrying the both of them upon its chest. Basia screams as she twists her blade, hearing the metal contort and crunch beneath her grief. The one thing she can do to grieve is enact violence on these constructions that took Hanka from her.

The second helm cracks like an egg, moonlight splayed across the ground. Two more Strażnicy eliminated. Yet, it doesn't feel like a victory. Nothing like the miracle of the stars floating into the sky takes place. There's an element of a ritual missing, and the storm in her mind begs her to consider what it could possibly be.

The pain in her heart, however, tells her not to worry about that.

All around her is soot and burning flesh. The flames lick at the walls too, but this castle is so old and crafted of such sturdy stone that she doesn't have to even consider setting herself ablaze as well. All she smells is ash and the acidic aromas that follow decomposition. The night-kissed construct never had a chance to live. The Strażnicy are dead. The night-kissed beasts are all dead.

And that includes Hanka.

Basia cannot look at her fallen body. She reaches for the stone within her breastplate. She knows she should save it for herself. She knows that the smart thing to do would be to find another person to act as a fellowship member whose only role is to ensure her resurrection. With just one Strażnik left to defeat, Basia would only need to keep them alive long enough that they can give her the sun's embrace and a second chance. Where would she even find another person? Stara Baśń? Would the Mistrz himself come with her to free the light? He worked so hard to free that town from the Kler, she doubts he would abandon that endeavor for something that would put him in immediate danger.

These considerations fall flat when Basia glances at the unburnt body. This is Hanka. Hanka, who has kept to her word of guiding Basia to the different places throughout the Kolebka. It would be a betrayal for Basia to leave her here and free the sun on her own. She also cannot spare the energy to carry Hanka's corpse throughout the Kolebka. The weight and the defilement will draw the Kler to her, as if destroying the Strażnicy hasn't already.

She should use the stone on Hanka, even if she is a night-kissed beast. If she tries it, she might waste the stone and leave Hanka more dead than before the enchantment—none of those creatures have been as human as Hanka has been.

But it might work.

Fighting back angry tears, Basia finds the pointed cylinder of stone and marches to where Hanka lies on her back. She'd be serene, if not for the tears through her body and the blood stains on her clothes. She is not waking up on her own.

Before sense talks her out of it, Basia grabs the resurrection stone as if it's a dagger. She screams Hanka's name as she forces it into her stomach. The stone smashes against her spine, breaking and expelling a light that is too bright even for Basia's trained eyes. She cannot let the pain and the headiness of the magic weaken her grip. The stone must turn from glittery to abyssal, depositing the entirety of the sun's embrace into Hanka's night-kissed flesh. The spell runs its course, covering Hanka's entire body in the bright magic of the sun's embrace. This luminescence chews through her clothing, leaving her naked but for the way the light obscures the many plains, hills, and valleys that make up the body.

The stone turns into a piece of dark matter. Light as a feather, it falls from her fingers. The squeal of more glass breaking makes Basia wince. Hanka doesn't move.

But this is the ritual that finally activates the moonlight captured within the Strażnicy. Tears stream down Basia's face as she watches the moonlight congeal into twin orbs which burst out and into the sky, freeing another Nadziemiec from the cage set for them by the Kler.

PART THREE: THE SUN

Chapter Ten

THE PROPHET'S CATHEDRAL

KAROLINA: SORRY FOR RUNNING AWAY

THE TWIN MOONS HANG heavy in the sky above Basia. Their light descends upon the audience chamber besmirched with the smoldering corpses of night-kissed beasts. Flames lick the bodies, sparks dance upon their now-torn flesh, and smoke billows from the cavities where Basia's blade had pierced them. For the first time since entering the Kolebka, Basia feels hot. The smoke around her carries heat, ash, and debris. So much destruction that might have been prevented if the Kler had simply kept to their promise of eventually returning the light.

Basia wipes the tears off her face as she looks all around her. So much ruin as far as her eyes can see through the pale moonlight, from the burnt night-kissed beasts to the fallen constructs, metal crushed and contorted in spirals that could only have been formed by flame and through the power she threw behind every swing.

Hanka's body, however, is the only corpse intact. A coating like white gold covers every inch of her flesh, covering her body and clothing like a shroud. Basia cannot even be sure what became of the wounds from the Strażnicy piercing her. Basia reaches forward—as a technomancer, the sun's embrace cannot hurt her. She removes her glove and tries to place her hand on Hanka. Stinging pain like the edge of a knife shears at her fingertip. She jerks her hand back, wincing and hissing.

It's not a phenomenon she had seen with the other resurrections. The delay between piercing with the stone and the dead rising took no time at all. The only light gracing those bodies had been that which stitched together the wounds, bright cherries of flame acting as healing. The shock had remained for a while, but it's already taken much longer for Hanka's light to go out.

Basia asked each member of the fellowship who had been touched by the stones what it was like to be resurrected. Only Marisia responded, and she had called it disorienting. She said the resurrection made her all too aware of the ways her body moved. The way her heart pounded in her chest and the ways her mouth responded to thirst and hunger changed dramatically. She mentioned never feeling warm again, more hollow than blessed by a magical miracle.

Basia feels that hollowness, and she's the one alive and grieving. Whatever sadness sits within the tightness in her belly is doused by the roiling waves of anger. It's insulting that the Kler's corruption of the technomancers' primordial creations is what took Hanka from her. Pitting one creation against another to try and extend this doomed endless night feels blasphemous. All because they were afraid of those first technomancer constructs becoming more than just magic and metal, while one of their own night-kissed beasts managed to become human. If they didn't let the technomancers' constructs achieve sentience, it's a cruel fairness that their own shouldn't either.

The Kler didn't intend for new life in their new world. They had no intention of delivering on their promise to return the lights as a reward for the decommissioning and the destruction of the pre-Zaćmienie constructs. If they wanted the world to continue in this nothingness, they succeeded, and she hates them for it.

She also hates them for making her alone in the Kolebka. They made sure of it by setting up so many obstacles to dismantling the darkness. It's more than one person can handle. There should have been thirteen of them fighting the Strażnicy together. They could have scattered across the Kolebka to the Kaplice and fought each of the Strażnicy simultaneously, hastening the return of the light to this world.

Alas, the only thing standing in the way of releasing the sun is a bereft technomancer filled with more anger than planning.

She exhales. Her breath leaves her mouth hot and heavy like steam. There's nothing more she wants than to inflict the same pain on the Kler as they have on her. They should learn the meaning of grief. The night's kiss is not holy. It's an abomination in the name of absolute power.

And she wants nothing more than to wrench it from them.

Basia rises from her knees, takes her sword, and leaves Hanka's glowing body behind with the spent resurrection stone lying beside her. From within the depths of her pack, she pulls out her notebook, looking at the drawings and notes Hanka had left behind for her. She draws her fingers along the path to the Katedra. It's the one place that might have something for Basia if she wants to bring Hanka back.

There might be some kind of antidote for having been embraced too closely by the sun as Hanka had been. It might also be a matter of waiting for the affliction to pass on its own. Basia lacks that patience.

With the twin moons hanging in the air above the Zamek, the Kler will know someone undid the enchantments holding back the Nadziemscy. They might descend upon the Zamek and the Wieża to investigate the destruction of their constructs. They might mobilize at the Ołtarz, surround the Strażnik Słońca, protect the last line of defense against the light returning.

Basia will not be able to bring Hanka's limp frame with her to Katedra Wieszczów. It might be better for them both if she doesn't.

With only the anger warming her chest and the vaguest memorization of a sketch in a notebook, Basia sets out towards the bastion of the Kler with no certainty if the Katedra will still be left standing by the time she has her way with it.

Basia runs along the Droga, following Hanka's meager directions to find Katedra Wieszczów. Much like outside of Tawerna, the lights lead uninterrupted to the bottom of the twinned stairs separated by a babbling river that glitters in the moonlight. It steals her breath to see such beauty. It's not all darkness, and there are even more things to be seen beyond the lights she carries. Pale green flowers and dark reeds dusted with frost waft in the gentle winds. She wonders what other types there are. Hanka deserves a bundle once the sun returns.

Basia wishes Hanka were alive, but she also wishes the bard could tell her what's at the top of the steps. All her notebook had were vague triangular points atop parallel lines representing towers. Basia cannot see through the night or see its kiss. She can only guess what awaits her here.

Beacons of light deposit golden glows in neat circles all up the steps. It's not quite the same as the Droga, but similar. Those are spaces to avoid if she doesn't want the Kler to be descending upon her. The last thing Basia wants is to announce her entrance. A technomancer should never be getting this close to their base.

In fact, the fellowship had agreed not to go anywhere near their strongholds unless they had to. And here, Basia climbs the steps of where they birth their beasts. She's already slept in the place that trains the Kler from novices to the fearsome magicians which uphold the darkness. Nothing scares her, not even the worry of what Hanka will think when Basia tells her of the visit to Katedra Wieszczów. It should pain her more to break that oath, but she's so distraught about losing Hanka in addition to losing the others. Tears sting in her eyes, and her feet hit the stone so hard, it's almost like stomping. These losses should sluice off her like water from a shower. Instead, they settle in her stomach like kindling, ready to ignite at the slightest provocation.

She pauses at a landing, squinting into the night. The stairs simply keep going, the lights from the lanterns not aiding anything in her visibility. What is the point but to keep intruders away?

The point is to keep her distracted so she doesn't hear the casting of a spell that encircles her in a collar. Her arms and thighs snap to her sides. Basia cannot call out, for who would come to her aid?

It was stupid to leave Hanka behind. Instead of giving into her own anger and frustration, Basia should have stayed there and waited for the poisoning from the sun's embrace to fade on its own. Or, if not that, once she had arrived at Katedra Wieszczów, she should have gone back as soon as she saw this colossal path leading to nothing.

Instead, she shrugs her shoulders hard and twists. The tether around her cinches tighter. She might not be going back to Hanka at all.

Fear grips her chest when she hears alternating the taps of footsteps upon the stone accompanied by the patter of a staff. She closes her eyes. She knows they likely won't let her live, but since they have her trapped, they should get rid of her. It'd be a mercy to put her out of her helpless fear and misery. Shards of night's kiss should be tearing through her body any moment now.

No such things come, only a voice that is almost familiar. "What do you seek, technomancer?"

She opens her eyes. Before her stands the priest who revealed Hanka's name—Patryk. Exhaustion pulls at his face, hollowing his cheeks and sinking his eyes. Those vertical pupils are pits as dark as the sky. Where he exposed his skin in Tawerna, he now hides it beneath loose clothing. The tattered cloak he wears is stained with some kind of wetness and hangs to his knees, clinging to his thighs. Is the return of the Nadziemscy something that would deplete the Kler like this? Basia hopes so. It means she doesn't have to kill them all herself.

"I don't want to cause you any harm." Despite his cold demeanor and stern face, Patryk has a voice so airy, it almost sounds like a purr or a plea.

He leans on a staff. As he shifts from one foot to the other, the azure jewels trapped within the spherical glass cage at its top twinkle with a pale blue, and Basia realizes it's the first time she has ever seen night's kiss when not cast as a spell.

"Let go of me," she grunts.

"Please, do not be frustrated. I mean no trespass. The Katedra rarely expects visitors."

"Well, I'm no visitor. I'm looking for something."

"The Ołtarz. I know what you've done." If Basia listened carefully, she might hear the pain in his tone. "I heard the cries of the Strażnicy as they fell."

"Why not kill me?" Basia cannot see the intention of her capture if it isn't to rid the Kolebka of the technomancers undoing the Kler's sacred work.

"You know where Hanka is, and I'd much rather not have her wandering the Kolebka by herself." He turns from her and continues across the landing.

She doesn't hear him casting, but her body rises, still trapped in the loops of his spell. Her toes cannot reach the ground. It's likely to make sure whatever defends the Katedra's entrance only hears his footsteps. That's how Basia would design it, should she have had the opportunity.

Patryk's magic pulls her along a straight path tucked along the side of the top level of the staircase. The night-kissed miasma glows along the Katedra's smooth masonry, the long slabs of silver slate uninjured by weather or time. It disgusts her to think that the Kler might have preserved their own architecture while leaving the rest of the world to decay.

She can turn her head and watch as the lamps of the stairs diminish behind her. There's no telling how far he's taken her, aside from her counting his steps, which she hasn't been. His cadence is far too uneven, and she wasn't ever much of a hunter.

Eventually, a door scrapes against the ground. Its hinges creek and Patryk brings her inside a building she can hardly see. Basia lets out a steadying breath. There's no light at all in this darkness, not for several moments, until she sees the rich, orange glow of natural flame. With its brightness, the tethers snap. She lands on her feet awkwardly.

The room's smell bludgeons her senses. Heaviness like salt fills her nose and the stinging taste of acid makes her mouth water. Something had gone rancid or died somewhere close. It might be under the table at the center of the room or under one or both of the nearby benches, but she cannot determine the source of this wretched rot.

"I do not have much time, technomancer." Patryk sits heavily at the table, leaning his staff against the wall. "Tell me, where is Hanka? She is not with you."

She stands across from him, not wanting to sit down. "She is resting." It's only part of the truth. "She got caught in the sun's embrace."

He opens his mouth, then closes it. The air within this tight chamber chills. "I see. And was that your doing?"

"It wasn't, I swear. It was an accident." Tempering her own intentions of coming to the Katedra makes her want to start shouting. Instead, she swallows her frustrations and says, "I'm looking for a way to undo it. I need your help."

"To undo the sun's embrace, or the Kler?"

Basia needs to burn the Katedra to the ground. "I was going to steal it. Whatever can heal her."

"You could have slaughtered a night-kissed beast for its blood, although it hurts to think about. The moons' light and the starlight make them quite lethargic." He raises a bony finger and taps it against its ear. "You cannot hear them, but they wail. Though, I think it is more mourning than pain. The Strażnicy called out for their kin."

Hanka didn't mention hearing any of the Strażnicy cry, only the night-kissed beasts. "The Strażnicy are constructs. You shouldn't be able to hear them."

"Ah, then it must be a connection between the Kler and their creations. Fascinating." Patryk shudders, bending forward, pressing a hand against his chest. After several rounds of breaths, he collects himself. "I would like to see the Strażnik Słońca, the mightiest of my kin. But I would so very much like to see Hanka again. Will you bring her to me?"

Without even giving herself time to contemplate, Basia says, "No. Absolutely not."

"What if I go with you?"

Beneath his cloak, he shivers, but his skin glistens. He has a fever. This priest is not well, and it's not for Basia to determine his sickness. "You seem to not be in any condition to be going anywhere."

"I cannot say you are wrong." He chews on his bottom lip and closes his eyes, dark lashes fluttering. "What if I tell you where the Ołtarz Słońca is, and you can bring me Hanka?"

Before she can answer, coughs wrack his throat, and Patryk braces himself against the table's rough surface. His cloak parts to reveal his chest and stomach, and she doesn't see the same flat planes of flesh she saw back at Tawerna. There are bubbles and bumps, bulging and turning his pale skin translucent. The scars already crossing his skin stretch as if to burst.

"Are you ill?" she asks him.

He waves her off. "It is none of your concern, technomancer. I have a duty to fulfill as a beast."

"Duty?"

"To the Kler. To the brood. Penance for my failure of letting Hanka escape. They wanted us to couple to see if we can make constructs that do not need any of the Nadziemscy's power. Instead, in the name of the dark, I play father to night-kissed beasts, hoping that another pair like she and I are born again." Trembling, he grabs the edge of the table tightly. With gasping breaths he stands, clutching to his staff. "I've told you how to cure Hanka. I ask that you leave. Let me continue my service in solitude."

He drags one foot over the other as he exits. His sluggish movements give her enough time to think of what she should do next. Many things in her mind and in her heart shout at her to leave. He's right, she can find another night-kissed beast to slaughter and hope its blood and flesh can wash away the sun's embrace that binds Hanka.

Instead, she stands still, watching Patryk slink forward into a narrow passage with faint white lights strung along the bottom walls. Everything about his movement suggests he will collapse soon. She cannot say she feels any pity for him. He should have followed Hanka if he wanted to be spared from whatever the Kler had planned for their night-kissed humans.

Curiosity prevails, and she keeps her distance as she begins following him. She holds onto to the hilt of her sword to angle it such that its blade doesn't scratch the ground. She doesn't want to attract the attention of any other priest. But with Patryk as weak as he is, the piteous sight might be enough to summon his siblings. With each step, she wonders if it would be a kindness to slaughter him. He hasn't given her directions to the Ołtarz Słońca, but that doesn't mean she can't figure out a different way. She's sure that the directions Hanka provided are more than enough.

The journey itself only lasts the claustrophobic distance of that narrow passageway, though it feels like it takes an age with Patryk's labor. At the end of the hall, with a great groan, he turns the knob on a metal door with a window decorated with evenly-spaced stars etched into its surface.

She should leave him, just be patient and let him complete whatever this duty is. On the other hand, she wants to supervise him and make sure he doesn't die. He's the only person who can help her in finding the last Strażnik, and all because of his love for Hanka.

Instead, she ducks inside, watching him as he collapses onto the wet floor shining under the lights hanging from the ceiling like ribbons. It reminds Basia of the Strażnik Astralny, but nothing confers cold. Instead, she feels her skin prickle into goosebumps as a clammy breeze blows like a breath against her body. It brings with it the reek of salt and brine, as if she dunked her head into her family's fermentation barrels.

A great figure glides along the floor like a snake with the segmented tail of something more crustacean. Unlike the night-kissed beast that had defended the Wieża, this one does not wear armor. Its slick skin glows purple with patterns like marble undulating beneath the thin membrane. Its color turns pale, almost white, as it travels up its torso carved like human muscle, the color broken only at the places where plates cover its flat chest and act as vents for its ribs. Lithe and slippery, it bears the most sickening beauty. Basia tries not to breathe too hard to protect herself from inhaling whatever spores and mucous float in the air and to stop from revealing herself through retching.

Patryk undresses, removing his cloak, his trousers, and his boots. The metal he wears stays on. His clothes fall onto the floor, revealing orbs painfully bulging from beneath his skin like abscesses, the shade of his skin a fierce purple like a bruise.

The night-kissed beast slides around him, scooping up his bulbous body. This creature barely fits in this round, cavernous cell. Its pointed face is almost human, if not for the carapace-like mask that shields its nose and chin. The way the lines in its face curl, Basia could almost say it smiles at him. Its black eyes narrow to bright blue pupils, examining Patryk.

Within its svelte, human arms, the beast turns Patryk around, holding on to him like a babe. His body leans backward, reclining into its cupped hand. Despite the heavy way he breathes and the repose taking him, his cock stands erect. The night-kissed beast takes a clawed finger and caresses its length. Its sharp point would be enough to draw blood. As he shudders through that dangerous tenderness, the beast takes another one of its claws and cuts into the protruding bubbles on Patryk's torso. Blood bursts from the incisions like mist.

Patryk moans, enraptured. The night-kissed beast doesn't let its digit off his prick. He moans and squirms as it cuts through more of the growths. The orbs and globules slide out of the incisions, spreading his skin and rolling down his front. The beast catches them in its lap, where they absorb into its skin.

The only sounds in the cell are Patryk's calls of ecstasy and the popping and plopping of those eggs. Basia cannot takes her eyes off the horror before her. This mutilation is unnatural, and Patryk, being a priest himself, allows it. What makes Basia's heart hurt most is this is the vision the Kler likely had for Hanka as well, and Patryk wanted to take her back to the Katedra to be imprisoned like this, to a life where they would be nothing but spawn beds until something like them appears again.

The beast stops cutting into Patryk when he shouts out loud. Whiteness spurts from his cockhead. He writhes within the beast's hold. It collects his cum into the same depression where the eggs had fallen into its skin. This is copulation between beasts and Basia wants to run away from it with vomit trailing from her mouth.

She stays, however, frozen in a fear she has never felt before. *She's* not the one in danger in the Katedra. The priests are a danger to themselves and the beasts they sired into this world. She hopes the return of the sun destroys them all. If it doesn't, she'll make sure her sword carves up each and every one of them.

Patryk trembles like a newborn deer when he finally stands on weak knees. His body sways as if inebriated. Blood trails down his chest and stomach. A crimson stream flows along his thighs. He looks past her as he ambles forward.

"I told you not to follow me," he moans. Shaking, he reaches for the handle to open the door.

Basia grabs it first. As she pushes it down, she takes Patryk by the neck and shoves him into the passageway. He braces his hands to stop from knocking his head into the wall, and she wishes he hadn't. She should have pushed harder.

"Did you enjoy that performance of my duty? The way I have offered my body to the night from which I was born?" His soft tone spits venom. He doesn't want her pity, and it's the last thing she wants to offer him. Though he curls into himself, he still towers over Basia. But she has a blade she's not afraid to thrust through him if he tries to use any of his magic.

"You wish I enjoyed myself," she says with a sneer. "Does every priest in the Kler give themselves to the beasts or is it just the night-kissed?"

"Just the night-kissed. We're made by the Kler, we should be giving ourselves back to the Kler to make the Wieczna Noc truly eternal."

Basia reaches back for the hilt of her sword. "I should just put you down right now."

"I don't think Hanka would like that. And I cannot tell you the location of Ołtarz Słońca if I'm dead."

"What do you want from me in exchange?"

"It's simple." He coughs then spits, black and red blood splatter against the floor. "Bring Hanka."

"Absolutely not." The words come quickly. She told Hanka she wouldn't be coming here on her own, and Hanka wouldn't be leading her to the Katedra anyway.

"Perhaps, I should tell you the location of Ołtarz Słońca, and you bring her to me there." His glassy blue eyes search her. Patryk's mouth hangs open, quivering into a sneer.

Basia should just kill him. She should tear him open with none of the delicacy that the beast just offered him. Thoughts of Hanka, however, stay her hand. This is her broodmate. He didn't attack Basia, only offered information in exchange for her not slaughtering the Kler. And she obliged. Despite bringing her, a technomancer and a weapon, into this sacred space, Patryk has not wished her any harm. He could have called for other priests. Instead, they all but ignore her.

She could murder him and lie. She could spin a yarn to Hanka about how dangerous he was. But looking at him now, she only sees a young man forced to reckon with travesties committed against his flesh. It's not her job to free him.

She cannot let Patryk take Hanka into this butchery with him.

"You know what I intend to do there, right?" She furrows her brows. Her shoulder aches from how badly she wants to swing her sword.

He searches her with the same cat-like eyes as Hanka's. "It was you who freed the moons and the stars. I should be impressed, and yet. You have no idea the terror you are willing to unleash upon the world."

"The terror is already here. Is what's being done to you not terror?"

"No, it's worship. It's ensuring the survival of this world, once the town's constructs have run their course."

The urge to kill him nearly overwhelms her. It would be a fitting punishment for this vile pride. "Your worship is a curse."

"This worship is what prevents the world from falling into utter ruin. It makes it so we have no need of the Nadziemscy. The night blesses us all. It's a shame that you want to undo it." He pants. His bleeding chests rises and falls heavily. Blood drips and drops against the floor. "Promise me you will bring me Hanka if I tell you the location of the Strażnik Słońca. I cannot go on by myself."

And Basia cannot bring the sun back by herself. The sole hesitation she has is the genuine worry that Hanka will take pity on this priest. She will see what the Kler had done to him and offer to run away with him, somewhere away from Basia, leaving her to fight the Strażnik on her own. Most of her disagrees. That departure seems doubtful. Much more likely is that if she tells Hanka what this plan entails, perhaps the bard will be amenable to playing along.

If she awakens.

"I will." Her heart beats loudly as she worries that he didn't hear her.

"Good." Patryk beckons her to him. She takes the handful of cautious steps towards him, tilting her head up to face him. The stench of sweat and sick billows from his parted lips as he lowers his head to her. She worries. Basia has already betrayed Hanka by disregarding her instruction to leave the Katedra well alone; she cannot also be kissing the man who all but abandoned Hanka to the Kolebka's wilds. Instead, he places his lips close to her ear and begins whispering. It must be enchanted; her tight grip on her sword loosens.

The spell he weaves into her ear is the way to the Ołtarz Słońca. His instructions are precise, telling her the distance along the Droga to travel, exactly what landscapes to look out for. He deposits gray images into her mind of the exact landmarks to find. The trail of statues of hooded Kler pointing the way forward through the woods and up to the mountaintop, each one kissed by night and invisible to those without the right magic. Only Hanka will be able to make out these markers—they don't stand anywhere near the Droga.

"I won't be able to see them," she whispers.

"No, but I've ensured that you will know as you approach them."

She lets out a shuddering breath. This type of magic is a violation. No one should be able to alter the thoughts within another's mind like this. "Have I been kissed by night?"

"It is a fleeting thing." He hovers for a little while longer, allowing the column holding up the Ołtarz to come into view. It is a cylindrical structure that rises high above the tree line, supporting a platform. Vines and flowers carved from stone and wrought from iron swirl up its length from its base all the way up. A pair of slab-like doors open, revealing a small platform not unlike a lift.

Basia breathes carefully, not wanting to sound too relieved by the lack of stairs.

"I will meet you at the top," are Patryk's last words before he pulls away, his back hitting the wall with a soft thud. His blue eyes glow like light reflected in water. Bliss washes over his face. His thin lips flatten into a gentle smile.

Through a clenched jaw, Basia asks, "And why shouldn't I kill you now? I got what I needed." The desire is there, but she cannot bring herself to exact such violence. Perhaps it is because of his physical torment at the hands of the beasts and the Kler. She's never taken on that kind of pity, however.

Patryk says with a sneer, "I'm not sure Hanka would appreciate that."

She resents how right he is. It's for Hanka that she is here. It's for both their sakes Patryk didn't take her deeper into the Katedra. But it's her fondness and affection for Hanka that stays her hand. If Basia kills him and lies, it will eat at her. If Basia kills him and tells the truth, Hanka will never trust her again.

Basia squeezes her eyes shut then opens them. "So be it. I'll bring Hanka to the Ołtarz."

Without waiting for his response, she takes off down the same passages and corridors Patryk had guided her through. With the way he pecked her with night's kiss, Basia worries that he can hear her thoughts. That he knows she has no intention of leaving Hanka with him, regardless of what Hanka wants.

If he wants to destroy himself in the name of the Wieczna Noc, he can do that on his own. He doesn't need Hanka at his side to share in that mutilation.

Basia's feet hit the ground hard, her footsteps echoing. Patryk doesn't call after her, and the congregation of Kler within the Katedra do not descend upon her. Even without the immediate danger, she flees, running towards the Droga's long stream of light as if the night nips at her ankles, ready to swallow her whole.

Chapter Eleven

RESURRECTION

BOGDAN: HE WAS THE BEST NEGOTIATOR

Air punches Hanka's lungs as if she's breathing for the first time. The violent inhale is disorienting, wracks her throat with coughs. She's never been sick before, but she knows she's seen this happen with people at Tawerna, the way their throats contract and their mouths expel saliva.

She's sick, and she doesn't know with what.

White glints in her vision like staring into a lantern for too long. The ache in her eyeballs makes her sockets feel far too full, but at least she has the heels of her hands with which to grant some relief. Her arms weigh heavy though, like a pair of sledgehammers. She's slept before, she knows aches and soreness can accompany poor posture and restlessness. The firm, stone ground holding her back straight might be the culprit behind this discomfort.

But Hanka also doesn't know what happened. She remembers the Strażnicy with their heads and faces replaced by the moon's smooth surface. She remembers the chanting and screaming of the other night-kissed beasts, though she doesn't hear them now. The quiet allows her to collect herself, but the pieces aren't around for her to pick up.

Did she die? Basia can't have let her simply fall asleep. That would be reckless and, as importantly, not part of their agreement.

It takes great effort, but she manages to sit up. The thing she notices first is that she cannot see past a meter or two in front of her. Her body glows, obscuring the darkness. She used to see grays of all brightnesses, but now, all she sees is either the color of an abyss or this uncanny yellow that seems to radiate from her skin itself. She slides a hand against her other arm, and it comes back wet and a little slimy. It's not blood or sweat, that much she can tell. She tastes it and its sweetness reminds her of honey. This affliction is not anything she recognizes.

Before she can begin to wonder where Basia had run off to, she hears footsteps pounding across the stone. She turns her head to where it's loudest, but without her vision, all she has to go on is the familiar silhouette and the shout that comes from across the space. She thinks it's the Zamek's audience chamber where they met the Strażnicy. It must be, unless Basia had carried her elsewhere.

"Hanka!" Basia trips over herself, sliding across the ground drenched in muck and other liquids Hanka cannot smell. Sweat draws clean lines down Basia's face. Droplets cling to her jaw. Others slide down her neck. She spits before rasping, "Thank the Nadziemscy you woke up."

"So, I did." Basia touches her face. Hanka's cheeks burn, not just from an unfamiliar fever but from the realization that all her clothes have disappeared. She looks to the ground beneath her. A dark corona of ash remains—that must be what happened to them. Did Basia do this? "You look...frightened."

Basia's skin has sunken into her cheeks and formed stains like bruises beneath her eyes. She swallows her breaths as if parched. "I am, I just returned from the Katedra."

Hanka raises a brow. "You went to the Katedra?" From her vague recollection of the maps, it's a considerable distance. The way Basia trembles suggests she ran hard and long and fast to escape. She should have rested. Instead, she can barely stay seated upright without vibrating.

"I didn't trust the directions we had. They're fine, but I was also so, so angry that you weren't waking up. I hated the thought of letting you die twice. And I met Patryk." Basia's eyes go wide and listless. She shakes her head to snap herself out of whatever hole she tripped into. "He said if I bring you to him, he'd tell me how to get to the Ołtarz. I'm so sorry to have used you as a bargaining chip. I won't protest if you want to stay with him. You gave me one direction, and I didn't follow it."

The physical pain dancing across Basia's face makes Hanka's heart hurt. There is so much guilt. And for what? If Hanka didn't want Basia at the Katedra at all, then she would have never given her the directions. It stings a little bit that she couldn't trust Basia to leave it alone altogether, but it's the same pain as an unexpected spark from wool clothing. Nothing to worry about. But there's something Basia isn't saying.

"Does...does the Katedra still stand?" It's the least Hanka needs to know.

"It does. Patryk caught me before I could really enter it."

"Then there is nothing to apologize for. What was your encounter with him like?" She wants to know what this Patryk long made a stranger is like. He clearly believes in the Kler, his religious fervor unabated.

"Hanka..." Basia gasps, breath stuttering. "I understand why you ran away. I've seen what they do to him. He's some sort of carrier, a vessel from which beasts spawn. I saw him—" Her cheeks puff out as she coughs.

The witch saw what Hanka had all that time ago. As the other half of the only pair of night-kissed humans, Hanka tried to warn Patryk of their intentions with them. She had seen what happens to the mature beasts—they wouldn't be honored for their humanity. The part that breaks her heart is that he gave into it. He's lost to the Kler, and there's only one way to free him from their influence and their grasp.

"I'm going to have to ask you to kill Patryk. I don't think I can bring myself to do it." Tears spill from her eyes. "If he really wants me by his side, he should have searched the entire Kolebka. I stayed in the Kolebka because I hoped he might try to find me."

"He was at Tawerna when we met."

"Yes, because he was searching for *you*. I only happened to be there. If I was what he wanted, then he would not have come in the company of four other priests. He should have come alone, and he *didn't*." Her voice grows thick with the sob she wants to let loose from her throat. "So, please, Basia. Put him to rest. It's the best for all of us."

"Of course, Hanka." Basia places a hand on Hanka's warm face. "There's already so much blood on my hands, what's a little more?"

Hanka gives Basia a sad smile as she places her palm on Basia's clammy hand. Both their lives have been touched by loss, but Hanka's is scarred more by absence than abandonment. She cannot imagine the wounds from slicing a sword into flesh; the injuries she herself left in skirmishes never felt malevolent. She has no enmity towards the Strażnicy. They had their singular role to perform. Hanka had no desire to stick to hers. If you can't escape, death might be the only way out, and it pains her that it took her so long to accept that fate for Patryk.

It gives her great relief that she won't be the one to snuff him out.

"How are you feeling?" Basia asks. "Can you stand?"

Hanka looks down at her naked body. Beads like dew glisten against her skin. It's a secretion; the sun's embrace weeps from her nascent flesh, enveloping her in a glow not unlike gold. She tries to move her legs, but they don't comply. Instead of being frustrated, she laughs. It feels good to see through the world's darkness and find the familiarity of Basia as her only anchor in it.

"I can't, but—" She reaches for Basia's singed scarf and pulls her into her chest. "I just want to stay here a little longer. To have you in my arms."

Basia whimpers, but doesn't try to shimmy out of the embrace. Instead, she wraps her cold arms around Hanka's waist. They stay like that for a few breaths. Basia is so cold, and Hanka wants nothing more than to share this excess warmth that feels like her body has turned into kindling. It doesn't itch, but it tickles, and the heaviness of the exhausted witch upon her dispels the discomfort.

Tenderly, Hanka combs Basia's hair with her nails, taking care to gently scratch her scalp. It's coarse with sweat and filth, and the one place she wishes the two of them could be is back in Stara Baśń's baths. The city had reeked similarly to the melted and charred bodies that litter the Zamek's audience chamber, but the baths had been clean. So close to Basia, all Hanka smells is sweetness and a musk like brackish water. She deeply sniffs the top of Basia's head and gives it a loud kiss.

This awakens something in the witch, who smoothes her hands against the slick planes of Hanka's sides and breasts. Her fingers press into the modest swells, pawing her way up to Hanka's nipples. She squeezes them between her strong, sword-gripping fingers, plucking at them like the Hanka would the strings of her balalaika—she doesn't see the instrument anywhere. As quickly, she remembers it shattering because her own foolishness suggested she use it as a shield. It didn't protect her, not in the same way Basia has.

Tenderly, Hanka pulls away if only to guide the witch's mouth towards her own. Instead of a furtive kiss, she teases open Basia's lips, prying them apart with her tongue. Instead of the sweetness cloying her throat, Hanka wants to taste Basia's mouth. They lap at each other, tongues slipping and sliding in a dance almost meditative. It's like they have all the time in the world.

They don't. Hanka knows they don't. Patryk is either holding Basia to her word or waiting for them at the Ołtarz, and there's no way to find out his itinerary.

Basia must have the same the thought, as she breaks their kiss first. "We should go to the Ołtarz. As much as I'd love to stay here, I've little interest in rutting among corpses."

"You're right." She'd be no better than the Kler, who conduct their breedings in nurseries all the time among the fallen bodies of beasts which never had a chance to be truly kissed by darkness.

"We should get you some clothes. You'll catch a cold."

Hanka stretches her arm out before her and looks at the shimmer along her skin like freckles. She twists it, observing. It's beautiful in the way the stars above are, but it will draw the attention of the Kler and other beasts alike. "I don't think it's the cold we have to worry about. But, please bring me my pack, if it hasn't been burnt."

"No, I made sure to keep our supplies safe from the flames." Basia leans back onto her heels and rises.

Movement still feels funny to Hanka. Her legs have the same structural integrity as the aspic served at Tawerna. Some solidity returns, but not enough that she thinks she can stand without toppling over. The last thing she needs is for Basia to fuss over her, not that she can tell that the witch has any nurturing instinct whatsoever.

Basia brings the sack over to Hanka and drops it onto the ground before her. Hanka leans forward, rummaging inside of it. She wasn't remotely as neat or meticulous as the way Basia packed her sack, but she had the benefit of planning and the consideration of the spent resurrection stones.

"I think it might make the most sense for me to carry the resurrection stone," Hanka says as she searches her sack for a tunic, trousers, and socks. She didn't have a second pair of boots to wear, and she wonders, with the warmth radiating from deep within her skin, if it matters that her feet have any protection at all. "Would you mind bringing it here?"

The witch crouches beside Hanka, hovering as if expected to help her dress. "I don't have it anymore."

"You don't...have it?"

"I used it on you. I thought that was obvious." Basia pinches the bridge of her nose and massages her tear ducts. "I didn't mean it that bluntly, I'm sorry. I just don't think I can bring the light back from the Kolebka on my own. I don't *want* to do it on my own. We're taking the world back from the Kler together or not at all."

Hanka's lips tremble into a smile as her fingers find the fabric she needs, starting with a tunic. She pulls it over her head. Immediately, the garment feels way too warm, like it's trying to bake her in all her body's heat and siphon this strange slickness. It's not right.

She rummages again, seeking the dress she had been given in Stara Baśń. She finds it and lets it fall against her body. It has no sleeves, but covers what it needs to. The tall socks they had also given her go on next. Rolling up the second sock to the tops of her thighs is when Basia's words about them only completing this profane task together catch up with Hanka. "That's precisely how I feel. Though, I am scared. No balalaika. These clothes are definitely not armor. I'm not even sure I have night's kiss on me right now."

As she lifts her finger to her mouth to chew it off again, Basia stops her. "Give me another chance to protect you."

Hanka nods. "I think I can do that." And it's with this that she stands. Her legs bow beneath her weight, but Basia rises to catch her.

"Once more into the Kolebka?"

"Once more into the Kolebka."

So, the two of them set off, seeking to put an end to this night eternal.

CHAPTER TWELVE

THE ALTAR OF THE SUN

ANIA: HOW COULD YOU HAVE BEEN AFRAID OF THE DARK IN A TIME LIKE THAT?

PATRYK'S VISIONS COME TRUE within Basia's eyes, remembered markings showing the way forward alongside the Droga. The stone statues of priests point her to the next section of the journey, so tinged with darkness that Basia isn't sure Hanka can see at all. They hold hands as they walked along the trail. Basia's legs still ache from running away from Katedra Wieszczów, even with the half tab of poppy leaving its dust along her tongue. Having the newly-resurrected Hanka on her arm, however, gives her the strength to keep going without pausing. Hanka herself seems to be in good health—a relief, as Basia never expected her gamble to work. The sun-embraced poisoning seems to be loosening its grip on her body. The strange dew beading against her skin has dried, but the warmth remains. It's like Hanka had never been a beast.

But it had been that very beastly nature that made her the best ally Basia could have asked for. Even without Hanka's powers over night's kiss, it's a relief she doesn't have to face the Strażnik Słońca alone. This last fight will be the toughest, but there's no fear tampering with Basia's steps.

She doesn't give any life to the idea that there's a possibility that she herself might fall. It's a useless concern. There is no means to bring her back; all the resurrection stones have been spent. Through the whispering, frosty winds, she hears them clinking against each other within her large leather sack. She should have left them behind, buried them in the snow in a makeshift graveyard. The weight reminds her that there will be no going back to her world before. The technomancers in the lands beyond the Kolebka have definitely noticed the thirteen stones missing. They would have noticed the fellowship's absence. If Basia were to return, she'd have to pay for those crimes, even if none of the planning had been her idea. There is no more backup. It's just her and Hanka against the Kler's darkness.

They don't say a word to each other as they roll along the perfect pavement to the foot of the Ołtarz Słońca. Even without the glow of the moons and the stars, Basia can see night's kiss all over its surface, shimmering and glittering like falling snow. She wonders if this is how Hanka sees the world, dusted with lights unseen to others.

"This is it," Basia says.

Hanka inhales deeply, then exhales. "And how are we getting all the way up there?"

As if answering her question, the slabbed doors that Basia had seen in Patryk's visions open, revealing a concentric platform with a large button in its center. The button isn't flat, but curved, like an orb with several closed eyes pocked along its surface. Arched rays like waves surround it, while carved into the rest of the stone are geometric stars far too detailed to resemble what now twinkles in the sky above.

Hanka reaches for Basia's hand. "Together?"

"Together."

Together, they step onto the sun's face. The stone groans as it sinks into the depression. The lift's iron gates wail shut as the platform shudders and begins its ascent. Hanka grabs onto Basia's arm. The witch pulls her into a kiss that she refuses to consider their last. With her resurrection, Hanka's lips are softer than they have ever been, and Basia wants to remember that softness. Hanka has a similar idea, as between kisses, she sucks Basia's lips between her teeth. They alternate gently nibbling at each other.

With the shortness of the dress Hanka chose to wear, Basia reaches below, her bare fingers skimming the fluffy hair between Hanka's thighs. The bard gasps, pressing her hips into Basia's touch as she dips her fingers between the damp folds, drawing gentle circles around Hanka's bud as their kisses become sloppier, looking more like an attempt to slake each other's thirst than showing simple signs of affection.

Hanka paws at Basia's waist. As much as she wants to undress, that satisfaction can come after the sun returns. Then, she will completely destroy the bard. She says none of this but curls her finger into Hanka's pussy and laps at her neck while the wind rushes past them. Hanka melts in her hands, savoring all the time this ascension affords them.

It's that promise of the future that ignites a new fervor for the fight deep within Basia's chest. The ache in her cunt will make her fight that much harder for a future with Hanka, a future that doesn't rely on artificially creating light for the world but on restoring its natural rhythms.

Hanka stumbles forward as she cums all over Basia's fingers. "Thank you, for everything," she says, breath coming out short and reserved.

Basia kisses her forehead. "We're not done yet." She winks and licks Hanka's honeyed slick off her fingers. Who knew the sun's embrace could make a night-kissed beast taste like liquid comfort?

The elevator scrapes to a halt while the two of them hold still with their breaths shaking. Basia knows that it's all nerves for her. She worries that Hanka will see Patryk, change her mind, and go back to him. The only assurance she has is the tightness of Hanka's hand around hers. Basia doesn't tighten her grip because she wants to spare Hanka from her own nerves.

The gates open loudly, creaking under the frost gathered on their curved surface.

Basia gasps at the sight before them. The Ołtarz is a large plaza at the far end of which is a glowing glass orb tucked into a seat like quartered bowl. The Strażnicy Dwóch Księżyców and the Strażnik Astralny with all its fabric wound as tightly as possible around its narrow frame would fit comfortably inside the orb with room to spare. Within the glass, pale purple molluscoid arms slither and crawl all over each other. It reminds Basia of the river eels popular throughout the enclave where she grew up. These wriggling limbs bump against several ridges within the glass that, if Basia didn't know better, remind her of fat pussy lips rather than the lids of any eyes she had ever seen. She's heard stories of the all-seeing sun; clearly the Kler put it to rest.

Its bright glow calls attention to the slaughtered Kler strewn about the plaza. Their limbs contort from grievous injuries and blood seeps into the mosaic tiles depicting a pale sky dotted with white clouds, staining them a muddy red. Basia swallows hard. The only survivor sits on the ground, cross-legged, his hands folded in his lap. His staff stands upright beside him, the cage of gems glowing faintly with night's kiss.

He raises his head towards them. Basia cannot make out his features, but her gut tells her it's Patryk.

"Oh, thank you for bringing her to me, technomancer," Patryk shouts across the plaza. Though the wind brings his words to them, they still carry that same meek intonation he had before at the Katedra.

Hanka feels heavy in Basia's hand as they begin to cross towards him. Quiet resistance but bereft of hope. "What happened here, Patryk?" the bard asks.

Using his staff to assist, he stands, wobbling on shaking legs. "I told them I wanted the night to last forever, much like our forebears. They did not agree."

Basia lets out a curt huff. "The night's already coming to an end."

"They too wanted to end it—with the moons and stars unleashed, why not also return the sun? But I cannot let that happen. We're too close to a true Wieczna Noc."

"Hanka, what does he mean?" She faces her companion. This must be some code between broodmates or teachings of the Kler.

The bard looks at her with eyes wide and pupils tightened to thin slits. She shakes her head. "I never would have thought the Kler would break the night if part of it had been unleashed."

She never would have guessed that the priests would forego punishing those who interrupted their eternal night. Basia expected a resistance, a battalion of priests wanting to protect the last thing upholding their darkness. The Kler should be standing against them, not felled by Patryk and his own night-kissed magic. He must believe in the necessity of the Zaćmienie, even if his sires and new brethren believed otherwise.

He brings his staff close to his chest. "It is not a plan they shared among the acolytes and novice priests. They feared our impulses and our conviction." Basia remembers the violence the Basni Mistrz rained down on his fellow priests; the Kler was justified in its fear. "No matter. The remaining priests are too far away throughout the Kolebka to stop me. You can try if you want."

Chants fall from his voice. Miasma billows from his staff, cascading against the ground like a fountain. It pools, then slithers into an abyssal band painted with bright blue shine. Patryk steps over it, and it creates a deep black dam rippling like a wall of flame. The head of his staff shines bright like a beacon. He reaches his hand inside the cage and pulls out a handful of the gems. Some clatter onto the ground. He throws the rest up into the air, where they float and separate from each other. They condense and sharpen into long spikes, their points tapping against the air like spears thrusting into an enemy.

"No!" Hanka shouts. Basia stops her from running forth. "He's going to destroy the sun!"

Patryk doesn't look at them as he says, "The world needs the darkness. Why not make it permanent?"

"Patryk, you're going to doom us all if you do that." Basia has never heard Hanka so distraught. Sad, yes, but not on the brink of despair. "What will it take for you to stay this madness?"

"Return with me to the Kolebka, where we can cherish and be cherished by this new half-night *she* unleashed upon us." He extends his hand but doesn't come any closer. Patryk waits for their approach.

Basia wishes she could skip this part. All she wants is to see the sun rise with Hanka. She doesn't want to fight Patryk to stop him from extinguishing the sun's embrace forever. Instead, Hanka douses the fear by clutching Basia's arm and hugging it close to her burning hot chest.

"I'm not letting you do that." She bends to press her head against Basia's strong arm.

The witch almost wants to cry.

Patryk bows his head. "As you wish." He grasps his staff's shaft and swings it in an arch above his head. Basia doesn't see what he summons.

Acting more than thinking, she shoves Hanka off her and casts rozpalić for what she hopes will be the last time.

THE MIASMA ABOVE PATRYK's head hardens into swords that take flight in unison towards the bard and the witch. Basia raises her sword, creating a shield of flame for the spell to crack and hiss against. He fires again, and again Basia blocks. It's a spell so familiar from their days in the nursery, not something that Patryk should be using against them, as more magic peels apart the Strażnik in its glassy cocoon. Hanka doesn't know how much time they have before there's no stopping the metamorphosis, and it worries her that Patryk has become so powerful. Something in his service and duty to the Kler must have restored him.

Either that or he too devoured several of his own to claim their miasma. Hanka would have done the same.

Basia swings her sword forward, casting fierce arches of flame at him. He blocks them with his own crosses. The crashing magic sends tremors across the floor. Hanka wishes she could be more useful, provide as much support as she did when they first fought the guard at the Wieża.

It's the witch's job to protect her, and she attacks with all the ferocity of someone who doesn't want to experience grief ever again. She runs towards Patryk with her sword moving so quickly and throwing spells in such rapid succession that she reminds Hanka more of a lantern. Patryk's magic conjures more weaponry, slabs of solidified miasma meant to break Basia's stance, wear away at her stamina.

Hanka needs to do more than just watch the fight between the only two people she has ever cared about, but Hanka can't let Basia put herself in danger of falling to Patryk's practiced magic. Try as she might, the sun's embrace upon her flesh gets in the way of her desire to reach into the miasma and access her magic. It has left her, and it will return one day, but she cannot wait. Without her own natural powers, only more miasma will beget miasma. There aren't any night-kissed here—the Kler's corpses are still only human, after all.

She looks to the enchanted flames of night's kiss flickering against the discarded gemstones around Patryk's feet. Perhaps she can devour those and use the power to take on Patryk.

Basia leaps into the air, swirling her sword around, crafting a vortex of bright, sun-embraced flame. Both Hanka and Patryk watch her, awestruck. Something must have made Basia so brave and so powerful.

But she can't stay as distracted as her broodmate.

Hanka hops into a run, crossing the plaza. Sweat soaks her feet as they patter across the stone. She pumps her arms, begging her body to move faster. She hears Patryk shouting behind her, but she's too focused on reaching the only other source of night's kiss on the Ołtarz.

A crash startles her. Stone cracks beneath Basia's blade and flame roars. Her strike missed Patryk.

The miasma blasts Hanka with cold when she gets too close to that obsidian wall. It stops her in her place, and it burns her skin as tries to push towards it. She's never experienced this kind of rejection. Perhaps the magic itself knows she doesn't want to be with Patryk anymore. The magic knows that she intends to interrupt it. She needs to prove to the magic that she is a part of it.

Patryk gains on her, carrying his staff in both hands. For the first time, Hanka believes he means her harm.

"I'm not letting you take her from me," Basia hollers.

He doesn't reach Hanka. Fire bursts forth from Basia. Like a whip, the flames singe the back of Patryk's legs. He cries out as he falls forward, dropping his staff. It rolls away from him as his body falls face-first, hitting the Ołtarz's decorated floor with a wet slap.

Patryk doesn't come any closer. Hanka dares not approach him, but she can see the spell's violence. The fire from Basia's sword burned away the back of his trousers and slashed through the tendons holding his calves to his thighs. There's no more movement for him, and instead of anger that he wanted to destroy the sun, Hanka only feels immense pity.

"You choose her?" Patryk groans as he tries to sit up. He picks himself up on his elbows, but he cannot bend his legs to kneel. Instead, he flips over, staring at the stars above as they emerge from the darkness.

"I did."

"Why? You were the only one I had."

Hanka crosses her arms. "And yet, you did not follow me, Patryk. I waited in Tawerna for you. And you never came. Because *you* chose her first."

Bitter laughter bubbles from his lips. "I did not choose her at all. I chose the Kler, and they sent me after the witch."

This priest lying before isn't the broodmate she had grown up with—far from it. Much like when they had been growing up among the other night-kissed beasts, he still seeks comfort from Hanka, afraid of the world. The beasts, constructs, priests, and technomancers had never scared her. He did not let himself experience that kind of peace. Instead, he gave into the terror that is the darkness, offered himself to it.

"And I'm not the Kler." Hanka gives Basia a shaky nod. He deserves to be freed.

"My mistake." He turns his head to the side to let himself see Basia approach with her sword ablaze. "Do what you must."

Basia lifts her sword and, like an executioner in olden times, brings it down heavily upon the center of his chest. Hanka winces as she hears his bones crunch beneath the blade. His flesh squelches. No words or cries of agony come out of Patryk. The way he resigns himself to his fate makes her heart crack.

She hates how the fire that catches onto his skin makes his flesh smell delicious. Her mouth waters and tears flow from her eyes.

Like a cautious prey animal, she approaches his fallen body. Hanka kneels and looks at his face, serene now that he will never reawaken. Her hands quiver as she reaches for his cheeks, wanting to feel his skin for the last time. He lays beyond comfort, but she wants to give him some of this warmth plaguing her. Her fingers touch his clammy face. It's a cold she's never felt on another night-kissed beast.

"We need to take care of that darkness," Basia says, voice steady. "I know you need to mourn, but—"

"Cut off some of his flesh," she says without stopping herself. The words make Hanka want to vomit. This hunger for magic reminds her that neither of them had ever been just a priest or just a bard—they were two creatures crafted by the Kler, who had never had any respect for anything they created.

Sword still aflame, Basia puts it aside and pulls out one of the smaller daggers from around her waist. It sinks into the crispy flesh. Neither of them says anything while Basia carves the meat. She had done this before, when Hanka asked for the flesh of the knight back at the Wieża. The witch didn't question her then. She doesn't now.

Basia hands Hanka a sliver of the warm tissue. It crackles like a dying flame, but even within that brightness, she can see night's kiss. She pops it into her mouth. Patryk's skin bursts between her teeth like the turgid skin of a ripe fruit. The taste sends shivers across Hanka's body; she swallows quickly.

The warmth from the sun's embrace dims as night kisses her, her skin prickling with goosebumps. The Kolebka is a cold, cold place, and the Ołtarz Słońca rises so far above it that the chill seems closer and fiercer. The wind whips at her face, despite the columns and statues serving as a fence or guardrail.

"Do you want more?" Basia asks. The hollowness in her voice does not match the pity crossing her dewy face. "I can cut off a bit more. If it helps."

Hanka nods to grant her that permission. She needs to feel the miasma coursing within her. The well is still regretfully dry.

Basia passes her a few more morsels. With each piece slipping down into her belly, cold blooms. Night's kiss has returned to her, and more tears fall, this time of relief. She pulls at the magic making itself known within her. It pools in her palms again, and a chuckle of relief escapes her throat. It's not enough to cast, but it's enough for the spell crackling in the obsidian wall to recognize its own kin.

Hanka wipes her mouth with the back of her hand. "Let's end this night."

Basia nods. Hanka's body sloshes she stands, night's kiss returned to her once more, a wet pool of magic burrowed deep inside her flesh, sluicing through her muscles. It travels to her shoulders, dripping into her hands.

They leave behind Patryk's cored corpse and dash off towards the wall of darkness. Hanka gathers the miasma within her palm. It billows through her skin, and she reaches forward. The cold fire laps at the magic in her palm, but with each undulation, it catches on her gift in the same way that drops of water gather together to create a puddle. She pulls her arm back, gathering the miasma unto herself.

From the corner of her eye, she watches Basia swinging at the darkness with her sun-embraced light, peeling it away into sizzling steam. It reminds Hanka of their first fight with the Kler. Tawerna seems so far away, especially here, at the top of the world.

As night's kiss gathers within her, Hanka lifts her right arm to cast it upon the suspended jewels jabbing into the surface of the Strażnik Słońca.

Her magic reaches around the gems like tendrils, latching onto several. Hanka pulls her arm back and twists. She drinks in the magic through her skin as she manipulates the strands. The gems sway, heavy in her arms, but very malleable. With a strong pull, she makes them crash into each other, shattering. Such fragile stones should not be holding this kind of power.

Steam billows all around them as the flames dissipate and the magic shatters. The fog of the wall Patryk cast smothers them like a snowstorm, thick and heavy. Whiteness obscures Hanka's vision, and her perception of night's kiss dwindles as well. Like a withering fireplace, its blue shimmer disappears. The flow into her left hand slows to a trickle.

The only way she can find Basia is by the way the witch grunts as she swings her sword. Hanka looks in that direction—there is none of night's kiss to be seen.

"I think that's all of it," Hanka says once her left hand has nothing else to siphon. The remainder of Patryk's presence in the Kolebka is gone as well.

Basia stops swinging, and Hanka goes towards her, following the orange glow of her sword like a beacon. She reaches out and finds Basia's shoulder. She holds onto it, finding in that touch the same comfort as grabbing her palm.

Another bright light pierces through the wetness hanging in the air, the rays cutting through the fog like scissors slicing fabric. Basia gathers Hanka behind her, shielding the night-kissed beast from sun-embraced light. Its warmth does not burn, but her eyes squint at the effort of trying to see anything. She cannot catch her breath either; the sun boils the water away.

They're both too stunned by the magic to make a movement and stand there in the crepuscular rays, waiting for this divine light to clean the Ołtarz of the battle between the night's kiss and the sun's embrace.

Chapter Thirteen

The End

HANKA: THE ONE WHO WATCHED THE SUN RISE WITH ME

When the fog and mist finally clear, all they see is the Strażnik Słońca's shell cracked like an egg. The light from the moons and Basia's flaming sword refract against its broken surface. Shards litter its resting place, some large and heavy enough to have broken the mosaic decorating the ground. Liquid drips out from the newly-formed chasm in the shell, revealing a void. Nothing sits inside. The tentacles that once danced within are nowhere to be found. The slits for eyes have also disappeared from the cracked orb. It reminds Basia of her charms—blank and empty without magic.

She doesn't think she imagined the creature nestled inside it. "You saw something inside the Strażnik too, right?" She doesn't want to cry. "There was definitely a thing trapped within that glass."

The bard scrunches her lips as if chewing. If the Strażnik broke, the thing inside it must have been freed. Unless Patryk used enough magic to kill the Nadziemiec trapped within.

Basia refuses to believe it. "Hanka?"

"Do you think he succeeded?" Hanka spits out. "He can't have succeeded, it's impossible to completely destroy a Nadziemiec. It's why the Kler built all this to seal them away. Destroying them would doom to world to something worse than the darkness."

Basia nods in agreement, laying her sword down and sitting beside it. "I guess we have to wait."

An incredulous chortle leaves Hanka's throat. "Wait?"

"The moons and the stars aren't always meant to be seen." She cranes her neck back, looking up at the celestial lights. She cannot believe she broke the jewels and constructs holding them back. They seem so unreachable, but she quashes the thought of how the Kler could have possibly put them away in the first place. It's not for her to know. In fact, she might drag Hanka to the Katedra so they can destroy all instructions on how to recreate this treachery against the natural order.

But the fight itself has left her. Her body aches from the battles, the magic, and the way her emotions churn within her. Exhaustion takes her; she wants this quest to be done. She has lost so much and traveled so far. She wonders what the rest of the fellowship would have thought of her recruiting a night-kissed beast as her final companion. In that crowd, she might have also balked at the idea, if it had occurred to any of them. But Hanka brought an understanding of the Kolebka none of the technomancers would have uncovered on their own. It's entirely a blessing.

Hanka sits down beside Basia and looks out across the plaza, out towards the black expanse of the Kolebka beneath them. There's nothing else to hear, only the wind whistling across this zenith. Basia listens for any movement from the lift. There's nothing there either.

Only Basia and Hanka at the top of the world.

The bard rests her head on Basia's shoulder. The witch reaches around the small of her back to hold her close, huddling for warmth while there's nothing left to do but wait.

"What do you want to do when the sun rises?" Hanka asks.

"When?"

"Yes, when. Not if."

Basia lets out a low hum, thinking. She had spent so much of her journey assuming she would die before or at the end of it, she hadn't even considered granting herself the luxury to consider what would happen after. She's certainly not leaving the Kolebka. Not any time soon, and not without Hanka.

She thinks of what they will do next as she asks, "Back at Stara Baśń, we talked a bit about responsibility. What's our responsibility now?"

Hanka thinks before she replies. "To live, I think. The problems that come with the sunrise aren't ours. The world the Kler had built was falling apart; even if we had failed, they would've wanted to complete our task anyway if only because the night proved impossible to maintain. Or there might have been more rebellion. Regardless, we freed the lights, and the rest is someone else's problem." She nuzzles into Basia's shoulder. "What if we went back to Stara Baśń. I'm sure the Mistrz would welcome us as heroes."

The thought is so light it makes Basia laugh. "You think so? In that case, he should offer a reward."

"Indeed. I think it'd be good to have a house, overlooking a square. A place with a big bed that we can share and a proper kitchen. I don't think I'd want our meals being prepared for us."

Basia thinks of her family's fermenting jars. "I miss cooking indoors, actually. I'd like to have more green food." The crisp crunch of lettuce and sharp tang of pickled root vegetables is something her mouth yearns for. Over the course of her travels, she's had enough of the savory dried provisions and the vile slush that needs water in order to be at all palatable.

Hanka sounds curious as she replies, "I'd love to learn. It was one of the things they didn't teach us at the Katedra."

"Because you were beasts?"

"Because everything there works in service to the Kler. They don't have to worry about their basic needs if they're the masters of the night."

The remnants of the Mistrz's rebellion flash in Basia's mind. "I wish them the best of luck once the people living in the cities and towns realize that they are, in fact, not masters of the night. But I suppose that's none of our concern."

Rather than reply, Hanka gasps. Then points forward.

Along the far horizon, the stars begin to dim, but instead of more darkness, the sky blanches into lighter and lighter blues, which give way to a pale orange. The color shifts slowly as a great whiteness rises to spread its rays across the snow-topped peaks and the frozen lands of the Kolebka.

Wordlessly, the two of them stare, enraptured. Basia has only seen depictions of the sun. On all of those there were only ever a handful of eyes on its surface, likely a limitation of artistic expression. As it crawls across the sky, she can see now the real thing is an orb whose edges and rays undulate like a celebratory dance. Swirling red eyes pock its entire surface.

The sun stares down upon a world which it has not seen for generations. Neither Basia nor Hanka can tell if it is as happy to have returned as they are to have its warmth beating against their faces as its rays bring forth a cornucopia of color that bursts from the forests, plains, and mountains of the Kolebka below.

GLOSSARY

- Baśni Oko (Bahsh-nee O-ko): "The Tale's Eye," the lake upon which Stara Baśń sits

- Baśni Mistrz (Bahsh-nee Meese-CH'): "The Tale's Master," not a Mistrz appointed by the Kler, but a rebel who seized Stara Baśń from their clutches and declared himself the town's ruler

- Gwiedzna Wieża (Gvee-YEZD-nah Vee-YEH-shah): "Tower of Stars," where the Kler sealed away the Strażnik Astralny

- Katedra Wieszczów (Kah-TEH-drah Vee-YEHS-choof): "The Prophets' Cathedral," the city that's the base of the Kler and the main nursery for night-kissed beasts

- Kler, the (Klair): "The Clergy," the priesthood which ushered in Wieczna Noc

- Kolebskie (Koh-LEHB-skyeh): Of or belonging to the Kolebka

- Kolebka Wiecznej Nocy (Koh-LEHB-kah Vee-YETCH-nay Noht-tsy): "The Cradle of Eternal Night," where the story takes place

- Mistrz, plural Mistrzowie (Meese-CH', Mees-CHYOH-vyeh): "Master," would be considered a mayor of a town otherwise, serves the Kler

- Nadziemiec, plural Nadziemscy (Nahd-SHEM-mee-ehts, Nahd-SHEMS-tsy): "Celestial," one of the three sources of lights that got sealed away by the Kler

- Nadziemskie Kaplice (Nahd-SHEMS-skee-yeh Kahp-LEE-tseh): "Celestial Chapels," the holy sites where the Kler locked away the Nadziemscy. Their locations are only known to the Mistrzowie who run the towns and the Kler's highest ranked priests.

- Nadziemski Strażnik, plural Nadziemskie Strażnicy (Nahd-SHEMS-skee-yeh St-RAHSH-neek, Nahd-SHEMS-skee-yeh St-rahsh-NEE-tseh): "Celestial Guardian"

- Ołtarz Słońca (Owh-TASH Swoin-TSAH): "Altar of the Sun," the plateau where the Kler exiled the sun

- Oświetlona Droga (Ohsh-SHVYET-loh-nah Droh-gah): "The Lit Road," a large highway throughout the Kolebka that connects all the enclaves of humanity, be it towns or cities

- Panie (PAH-nye): "Sir" in English

- Rozpalić (Rohs-PAH-leech): "To light aflame," one of the spells Basia uses, it shrouds her sword in sun-embraced fire

- Rozpal ich wszyscy (Rohs-PAHL eekh vy-SHYST-tseh) "Light them all aflame," a more devastating version of the spell

- Smacznego (Smahtch-NEH-goh): The Polish equivalent of "Bon apetit!"

- Stara Baśń (Stah-RAH Bahsh'n): "Old Tale," one of the cities in the Kolebka, where the Kler trains its priests in combat and magic

- Strażnik Astralny (St-RAHSH-neek Ahs-TRAHL-neh):

"Guardian of Stars," one of the constructs built to hide away the stars

- Strażnik Dwóch Księżyców (St-RAHSH-neek Deh'VOOHK Kshehn-SHYH-ts-oof): "Guardian of the Twin Moons," a pair of conjoined constructs built to seal away the moons

- Strażnik Słońca (St-RAHSH-neek Swoin-TSAH): "Guardian of the Sun," a large construct which holds the sun

- Strażnicy (St-rahsh-NEE-tseh): "Guardians," plural of STRAŻNIK

- Szczyt Świata (Sh-CHIT Sh-VEE-ah-tah): "The Tip of the World," the name of the plateau that got turned into Ołtarz Słońca

- Tawerna (Tah-VAIR-nah): "Tavern," one of the towns with the Kolebka, where the story begins

- Technomancer: the class of witches who can wield light magic, a skill they call being sun-embraced

- Wieczna Noc (Vee-YETCH-nah Nohts): "Eternal Night," the state of the world without the sun, the moons, and the stars

- Wyjaśnić (vyh-YASH-neetch): "to brighten," another spell of Basia's, it enhances fire already present, weaker than rozpal ich wszyscy

- Zaćmienie (Zahtch-MEE-EHN-nyeh): "Eclipse," the name of the event that sealed away the sun, the moons, and the stars

- Zamek Dwóch Księżyców (Zah-MEK Deh'VOOHK Kshehn-SHYH-ts-oof): "Castle of the Twin Moons," where the Kler sealed away the twin moons

ACKNOWLEDGMENTS

Grief isn't easy. It comes and goes, and what closure looks like varies from relationship to relationship. I thought I got it when I went to the celebration of life ceremony for Rekka in September 2023. What I actually needed to do was transform 2017's *A Kingdom Calls to Me* into 2024's *The Cradle of Eternal Night* in their memory. I'm incredibly proud of this work, and closure is finally mine. Thank you, Rekka, for having encouraged me to self-publish and all the support you gave in the years we had together. I miss you dearly and love you just as much.

It would be negligent, however, to not give thanks to the living.

Thank you, Pom, for the beautiful art and the fulfilling collaboration. I hope we get to work together again.

I am grateful to N. Feeman for understanding what I needed between a line edit and a copy edit. It helped me realize just how difficult to execute this story has been. Thank you for showing me how much I've grown as a creative in the last seven years.

Shout out to Soren Häxan for helping me wrangle the cover copy. It's much stronger than any query I have ever sent.

To every beta reader since 2017, thank you for reading the various iterations of this story.

To the queerdo writers, thank you for being there for all the meltdowns and all the wins. I promise I won't intentionally plan to release two books in one year again to spare us all from the agonies.

With *The Cradle of Eternal Night* finally being in your hands, dear reader, the querying chapter of my author career officially comes to a close. It's all new work intended for self-publishing from here on out.

About the Author

Ladz was born in Poland, raised in New York City, and currently lives in Texas. When they're not a marketing manager for a major digital publisher, they're writing dark fantasy that tends to straddle other genres like true crime and horror. They can be found online at ladzwriting.carrd.co or on Twitter/Instagram/TikTok @ladzwriting.

About the Illustrator

PomPoison is a multidisciplinary artist making comics for adults. You can read his comics, view his illustrations, and see his recent work and words on his comic website littledeathcomic.com. You can purchase his digital comics on itch.io and physical pieces in the shop.

Follow him on social media: https://linktr.ee/pompoison

ABOUT ROBOT DINOSAUR PRESS

Robot Dinosaur Press features queer, inclusive science fiction, fantasy, and horror books from a collective of global authors. For an introduction to our work, sign up to our newsletter at robotdinosaurp ress.com/newsletter and receive a free anthology of short stories by RDP authors.

Also from Robot Dinosaur Press

The Peridot Shift by R J Theodore

In this Science Fantasy trilogy, a scrappy group of outsiders take a job to salvage some old ring from Peridot's gravity-caught garbage layer, and land squarely in the middle of a plot to take over (and possibly destroy) what's left of the already tormented planet.

The Phantom Traveler by R J Theodore

When one of Ehli's bantam sisters turns up dead, she tries to figure out what happened before she's blamed for the murder, and before the real killer strikes again.